Lottie Deno

The cover is from the painting "California Salt" by Benjamin Chambers Brown (1865-1942). The artist was born in Marion, Arkansas, and became a well-known California Impressionist landscape painter. His works can be found in the Smithsonian Institution, British Museum, Library of Congress and many other prominent art collections. "California Salt" resides in the author's private collection.

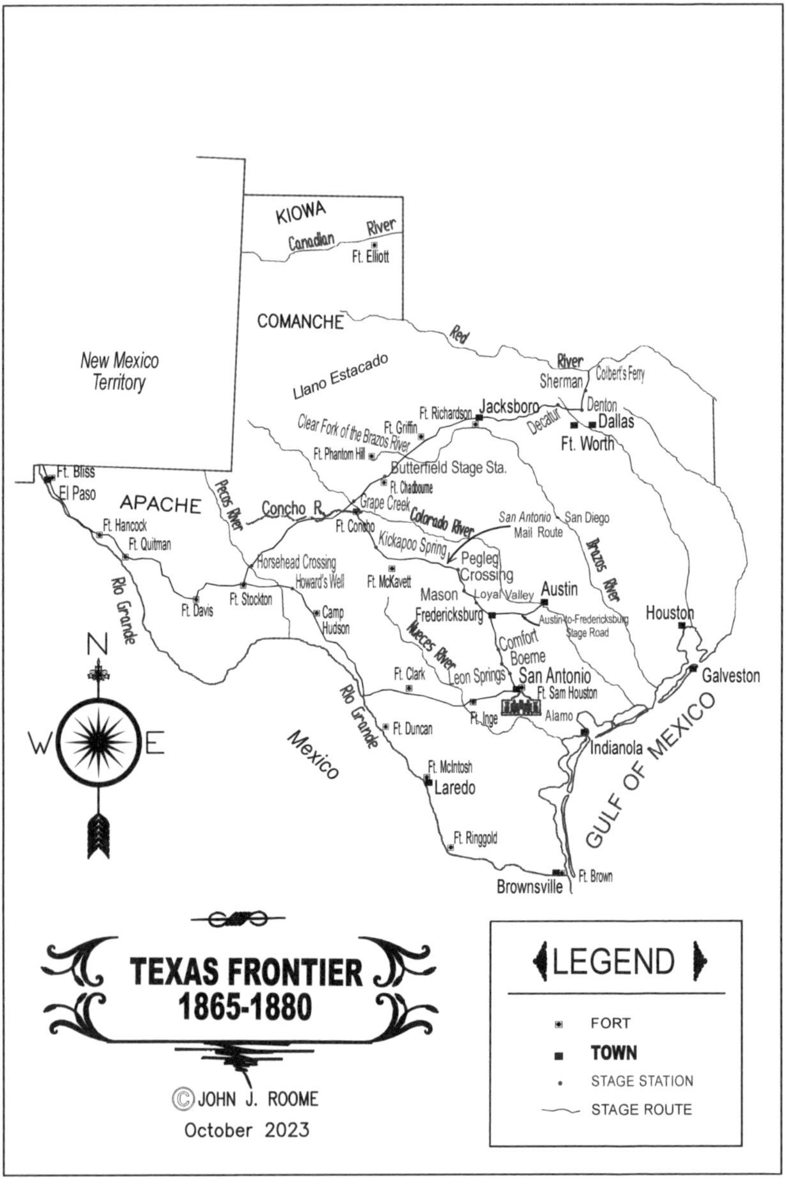
KIOWA
Canadian River
Ft. Elliott
COMANCHE
Red River
New Mexico Territory
Llano Estacado
Sherman
Colbert's Ferry
Denton
Jacksboro
Ft. Richardson
Decatur
Dallas
Ft. Worth
Ft. Griffin
Clear Fork of the Brazos River
Ft. Phantom Hill
Butterfield Stage Sta.
Ft. Chadbourne
Ft. Bliss
El Paso
APACHE
Pecos River
Concho R.
Grape Creek
Colorado River
Ft. Concho
Kickapoo Spring
San Antonio Mail Route
San Diego
Brazos River
Ft. Hancock
Ft. Quitman
Horsehead Crossing
Howard's Well
Ft. McKavett
Pegleg Crossing
Mason
Loyal Valley
Austin
Rio Grande
Ft. Davis
Ft. Stockton
Camp Hudson
Fredericksburg
Austin-to-Fredericksburg Stage Road
Houston
Nueces River
Comfort
Boerne
Galveston
N
W
E
Ft. Clark
Leon Springs
San Antonio
Ft. Sam Houston
Ft. Inge
Alamo
Rio Grande
Ft. Duncan
Mexico
Indianola
GULF OF MEXICO
Ft. McIntosh
Laredo
Ft. Ringgold
Ft. Brown
Brownsville
TEXAS FRONTIER
1865-1880
© JOHN J. ROOME
October 2023
LEGEND
FORT
TOWN
STAGE STATION
STAGE ROUTE

LOTTIE DENO

A Novel of the Civil War & the American Southwest

FRANK THURMOND

PARKHURST BROTHERS PUBLISHERS

Parkhurst Brothers Publishers
MARION, MICHIGAN

www.parkhurstbrothers.com

Consumers may order Parkhurst Brothers books from their favorite online or brick-and-mortar booksellers, expecting prompt delivery. Parkhurst Brothers books are distributed to the trade through the Chicago Distribution Center. Trade and library orders may be placed through Ingram Book Company, Baker & Taylor, Follett Library Resources, and other book industry wholesalers. To order from Chicago Distribution Center, phone 1-800-621-2736 or fax to 800-621-8476. Copies of this and other Parkhurst Brothers Publishers titles are available to organizations and corporations for purchase in quantity by contacting the Special Sales Department at our home office location, listed on our website. Manuscript submission guidelines for this publishing company are available on our website.

Printed in the United States of America

First Edition, February 2024

Printing history: 2027 2026 2025 2024 8 7 6 5 4 3 2 1

Library Cataloging Data
1. Author–Thurmond, Frank, American academic and author
2. Subject–Fiction, Americana featuring female roles
3. Subject–Westerns "Based on a true character"

2023-trade paperback and e-book

ISBN: Trade Paperback 978162491--204-7

ISBN: e-book 978162491-205-4

Parkhurst Brothers Publishers believes that the free and open exchange of ideas is essential for maintaining our freedoms. We support the First Amendment of the United States Constitution and encourage all citizens to study all sides of public policy questions, making up their own minds.

Cover and interior design by Linda D. Parkhurst, PhD
Acquired for Parkhurst Brothers Publishers and edited by Ted Parkhurst
Cover art by Benjamin Chambers Brown (1865-1942)

022024

To my Dad,

Frank Russell Thurmond,

in gratitude

Contents

Also by Frank Thurmond

Nonfiction:
Before I Sleep: A Memoir of Travel and Reconciliation
(Et Alia Press, 2012)

Fiction:
Ring of Five: A Novella and Four Stories
(Et Alia Press, 2015)

Poetry:
Remembrance and Other Poems
(Braddock Avenue Books, 2022)

Edited by Frank Thurmond:
Tales of the Arkansas Frontier, by Jon David Cash
(Parkhurst Brothers Publishers, 2024)

PROLOGUE

The Quest

THE SECOND TIME I NEARLY GOT SHOT was the day John Henry "Doc" Holliday showed up. It was a busy night at the Bee Hive Saloon in Fort Griffin, Texas, on a crisp spring evening in 1868. For certain reasons I will return to later, I had found myself there following a time of drifting after that unfortunate incident in San Antonio. (I will come back to that, too.) But there I was at the Bee Hive, just minding my own business flipping the pasteboards at my Faro table when in walked Doc.

I had seen him wandering around town, drinking and gambling among the nearly twenty saloons there in the Flat—as they called that godforsaken place—and I knew it was just a matter of time before he stumbled into the Bee Hive. And he did. Not long after he did, I found myself staring down the wrong end of a long-barreled Colt "Peacemaker" revolver—at the end of which were the furious eyes of a woman seething with jealous rage. What happened next must wait for later in my story.

Yet that was just one of the many close calls I had during my adventures in what they now call the "Old West." How I got to be there in the first place (and why I came to be called "Lottie Deno") is a tale unto itself. But it was all the result of meeting—and then losing—the man whose love would lead me on a search across the wild and perilous Texas frontier. That quest for true love became my lodestar, and I dared many a danger to find it again.

This is my story. Leastways my account, as I like to tell it.

PART I

The Golden Boy

1

MY TALE BEGINS IN KENTUCKY, on a large plantation near the small Ohio River port town of Warsaw in Gallatin County. I was born in 1844 on the twenty-first of April. (That makes me a proud Taurus, and I have always lived up to it.) They called me Charlotte J. Tompkins at birth, though I went by Carlotta and have sported quite a few different sobriquets in the years since. My parents were relatively well-to-do and owned (though I am now terribly ashamed to admit it) a large number of enslaved people. One of these plays an important part in my story: Her name was Mary Poindexter, a young woman who was assigned my nanny at birth and who would later become my closest friend and confidant—not to mention my protector on our many adventures together—in a friendship that would endure long after she finally obtained her free papers.

My parents' wealth in those antebellum years came from selling the tobacco and hemp crops they farmed on the plantation. My father was also a prominent turfman and owned a race track (renowned as being among the finest in the Bluegrass State) where he bred horses. He owned a stable of blooded racehorses that regularly won in many top sweepstakes. (He later gained some notoriety by serving in the Kentucky General Assembly during the War.) Being the older of my parents' two children, both girls, I reckon Daddy thought of me in a way as the closest thing he would ever have to a son and heir. So maybe that is why he took me along on most of his business trips to Detroit and New Orleans to sell tobacco and hemp—and even overseas to England and continental Europe to buy and sell horses.

Mary Poindexter came with us on those trips to keep an eye on me as my nanny. On those journeys, I saw Daddy in action as a gambler when he took me with him to many of the most famous casinos in the world. My father could hold his own with some of the most notorious gamblers of the day. I owe a great debt to my father for teaching me to "flip the pasteboards" (along with all the tricks of the trade he knew) when I was still just a young girl. By the time I was sixteen, I could play cards—especially poker—and hold my own with the best of them. I learned quickly that a man does not take kindly to getting fleeced by a woman at cards—especially a young girl! So I was very lucky to have Mary Poindexter always there to watch over me. Being almost seven feet tall and quite stout, she presented a formidable presence as she loomed over my shoulder and glared at all the men around the table. And she could intimidate the meanest of ruffians with a mere flash of her feared "evil eye."

My parents sent me to be educated at a local Episcopal convent, an exclusive finishing school for young ladies, where I learned to read and write (no small gift for a girl in those days) and was schooled in all the requisite Southern manners and social graces. These would set me apart as a lady with genuine Southern charm on the rugged western frontier where I one day wound up.

In the meantime, with all those beautiful thoroughbreds around our plantation and racetrack, I took up riding as a young girl. It was when I took up later with one of Daddy's jockeys that my adventures truly began. He was a boy called Johnny Golden, and meeting him changed my life forever. Though for better or worse, I still cannot say.

I first met Johnny during the hot and humid summer months of 1860. A harsh winter had been followed by the loveliest spring I could remember. The plantation was abuzz with activity, with all the hundreds of field hands (Daddy's euphemism for his many slaves) laboring from first light until dusk, harvesting his crops in time for shipping upriver to Detroit and down to New Orleans. Little did we suspect this would be our last such summer.

Yet for now, I was home from school, bored, and feeling a bit mischievous as I crossed the fields toward the racetrack to see what might be afoot amongst Daddy's jockeys. The late afternoon sunlight gleamed golden over the fields as I sauntered carelessly down the old dirt road leading from our palatial house, all but oblivious to the hundreds of sweating bodies on either side straining to twist the cotton from each individual boll out of millions as far as the eye could see. Later in life, I could never look at a single bale of cotton again without remembering all the toil and suffering Daddy's "field hands" had to go through just to prepare one of the thousands of bales that would eventually fill up entire barges at the river port. However, my adolescent mind was preoccupied with other things, principally those handsome jockeys I knew would now be exercising the horses at the track. I also knew what they usually got up to when they took their afternoon break, and today I had a plan. More like a scheme, you might call it.

Just as I had hoped, when I got to the track a small group of jockeys—all boys around my own age—were sitting cross-legged on the ground near the stables. They were playing poker, using matchsticks for money. One of them looked up as I approached, and when he saw me skipping carefree along the track in their direction, he dropped his cards in surprise and jumped to his feet. The other boys quickly followed suit. I must have been some sight, too, with my ginger ponytails trailing in the wind behind me over my white dress shining in the sunlight. The boy who had first seen me politely removed his cap and grinned sheepishly. I could not recall seeing him before.

"Hello, Miss Tompkins," he stammered. I was surprised at first that he knew my name. But then, who on the plantation did not already know everything there was to know about my family? Especially Master Tompkins' eldest daughter, whom everyone referred to as "Daddy's girl."

"Hello. And you are?"

"My name's Johnny. Johnny Golden."

"Johnny Golden," I repeated thoughtfully. "With the golden smile." I winked at him and noticed him blushing. He quickly looked away. Then I remembered where I had heard his name before. Daddy spoke over dinner that week about the new young jockey he had hired, saying Johnny was from a wealthy Jewish family in Boston with whom Daddy had done some business. They asked him as a favor if he would take on their youngest son at the track for the summer. The boy loved horses and riding, and with his slight build, they reckoned he might find good work as a jockey if he could learn the art of racing. He was also Jewish! I had never met an actual Jewish person and was intrigued to meet him. Little did I know the peril this would entail.

I asked the boys if I could join them at their game, and they at once broke out in laughter. But I sat down defiantly, crossed my legs, and nodded at the pile of cards. The boys looked at one other with bemused expressions before sitting back down and dealing me a hand.

We played all the rest of that afternoon. When I finally got up to leave as dusk was setting in, I had a mound of matchsticks piled up in front of me. I had won the whole pot.

When Daddy once caught me playing cards on the sly with servant boys behind the house, he had a conniption fit. He liked to have given me a whipping, too, if I had not put my long legs to good use and run as fast as I could into the plantation field beyond the outhouse. He drew a strict line when it came to socializing with the "darkies," as he called them. He expressly forbade it except with Mary Poindexter, my nanny since childhood. He seemed to turn a blind eye to my fondness for her, even friendship for my part (though the older I got, the more I wondered how she really felt, having no choice in the matter). But Daddy knew how useful (even indispensable) Mary was when it came to looking out for me—especially on all those trips he took me on—and so made an exception in her case.

But Daddy had not said anything about visiting the jockeys at the track, and I figured what he did not know would not hurt him. So I spent the rest of my afternoons that summer over at the track, honing my card-playing skills with Johnny Golden and the boys, while Mary kept watch on the road just in case Daddy might come home early from his business in town. I did not want to take any chances with his unpredictable temper.

One day, however, he did come back early. And, naturally, it had to be the day Mary was put to work helping Mama back at the house. Daddy decided to stop by the track and check on the horses. It was a lovely late summer afternoon, and he wanted to take his favorite horse, a thoroughbred mare named Ginger, out for a ride. The boys and I were taking a break from our daily battle for matchsticks (which I most always won). It was time to feed the horses, and Johnny invited me to make the rounds with him. There was something about Johnny and his winsome smile that I had taken a shine to. He seemed more mature than the other boys, even the older ones. Anyhow, I reckon I was starting to like him, though maybe I did not quite realize that.

One of the horses under Johnny's charge happened

to be Ginger, and we had just entered her stall when I heard Daddy's voice approaching outside. Something told me I should try to hide and keep my visits to the track secret. He was telling one of the other boys of his intent to ride that day when he walked in and saw me awkwardly trying to crouch in a dark corner behind Ginger. This was a foolish thing to have done on my part because it only added to his suspicions about my presence at the track. But as I learned that night at dinner, his suspicions now centered around Johnny.

"What were you doing down at the track today, Missy?" Daddy was staring at me across the table with stern eyes. Mama looked up surprised, while my little sister Ellie Mae giggled.

"We were just feeding Ginger, Daddy."

"But why were you there in the first place?"

"Well, I just ..." I paused a moment, trying to think up a good alibi, when Ellie Mae saw her moment to stir up trouble. She had just turned thirteen, and she often tended toward the mischievous.

"Carlotta goes there just about every afternoon, Daddy. Don't you, Carlotta?"

Mama shot Ellie Mae a look. "That's enough from you, young lady."

"Yes, ma'am." My sister giggled again as she waited gleefully for Daddy's (and my) reaction. I remembered the old saying that "honesty is the best policy" and decided to put it to the test for once. Trying my best to ignore my sister, I attempted a feeble smile at Daddy.

"I go there to play cards with the jockeys. They like to play poker with matchsticks during their afternoon break and let me play with them. I wanted to practice all those tricks you taught me!"

Mama looked at me concerned, while Daddy just sat still and expressionless. Ellie Mae looked like she was about to offer further comment but mercifully stayed quiet.

Daddy asked again, "What were you doing with the Golden boy alone in the stable?"

"Just helping to feed Ginger, as I said. What's wrong with that, Daddy?"

"I won't have you cavorting with no Jew boy!" he said firmly. This took me by surprise. I did not understand what I had done wrong.

"What's wrong with Johnny?" I protested. "I thought you did business with his family in Boston."

"Business, yes, and strictly that. That's all the Jews are good for. But I will not have my daughter gallivanting around my track with one."

"But Daddy!"

"You do not associate with that boy further, you hear? You need to find a nice, rich, Southern, and Christian boy like us who will marry you and help manage this plantation one day when it's yours."

"Yes, sir," I blurted, then suddenly scooted back my chair, rushed from the table upstairs to my room, and slammed the door.

Summer ended soon after that, and I packed my bags for school. I felt a strange mingling inside of both joy and melancholy: happiness at the approach of fall and learning at school, yet sadness at the thought of Johnny and the too abrupt end of carefree days playing cards and feeding the horses with him. Daddy had not said another word about it, but he had set Mama to keeping an eye on me to ensure I never found occasion to sneak off back to the track. I wondered what Johnny thought about my disappearance after that, or if he suspected Daddy's attitude toward him and his family just because they were Jewish. I still had much to learn about the world.

For now, I sat down at the desk in my room and wrote a letter to Johnny explaining what had happened and why I did not come back. (Though I did not repeat what Daddy had said about him and his family being Jewish.) I gave the letter to Mary for safekeeping until she could get to the track one day to give it to him.

In the meantime, I returned to school and resumed my studies in earnest. But I could not help seeing in the back of my mind Johnny Golden's smile and the new sensation of physical excitement I felt around him—or even just thinking about him. Maybe that is why I volunteered for the role of Juliet in our school play that fall. Acting out that scene where she must confront a similar situation with her own father felt rather cathartic. I knew just how she felt, and Juliet's plight helped me see that I was not the only girl in the world whose choices were confined to a father's whims (or prejudices). But while my own Romeo—as I now started imagining Johnny—was not exactly banished, he might as well have been considering what happened that next April just before my seventeenth birthday.

It was on the twelfth of April in 1861 when Confederate soldiers fired on Fort Sumter down in Charleston.

Our world and our entire way of life would soon be forever shattered.

2

BY THE TIME I GOT BACK HOME in early June, there was much excitement and hubbub around the plantation. At first, I hardly recognized the place. Our house had become a recruitment headquarters for the Confederate cause, and bright red and blue Rebel flags now flapped in the breeze above the front portico. Even though the Kentucky legislature was neutral and would soon vote to support the Union, there were just as many Southern sympathizers as not. Daddy was one of them. He had argued vociferously as a member of the state legislature to advocate secession, though a general desire for neutrality had overruled him. Daddy's reaction was to be among the first to volunteer for the newly formed Confederate army, and because of his status, he was given his own company to command.

Daddy represented a sizable faction of landowners like himself who could not foresee a profitable future for his crops without the continued use of forced, enslaved labor. He was a quintessential Southerner of the time. Somewhat ironically—and hypocritically too, as I now see looking back (though nobody seemed to notice it then)—there was constant talk of the constitutional right to freedom. But "freedom" in their minds clearly applied only to wealthy, white (and male) landowners like themselves. Everyone else, not only enslaved people but Indians, immigrants (overlooking the fact that all of us were, after all, once immigrants too), Jews, and Catholics—fellow Christians as they were—could rot for all they cared. Even poor Protestant whites were frowned upon, though tolerated as far as they could be manipulated to spend their blood (and later their votes) to the extent that even now—in the 1920s—these same wealthy elites perpetuate a nostalgic myth of "the Lost Cause" and the fantasy of some supreme, God-given white male privilege. (For my own part, I was then too young and naïve to comprehend the pure evil of slavery, as I later came to understand it.)

Yet they managed to rile up others to fight for them, too, including the same people I knew they otherwise despised. One of these was Johnny Golden. I had spent my first few weeks back home waiting for any chance to slip off to the track and try to find him, when to my great surprise, he turned up one day at the house at a reception Daddy was hosting for his new regiment. He was wearing a smooth gray Confederate uniform, complete with white gloves, shiny black boots, and a long sword by his side.

I knew Daddy had his eye on me, so I waited as patiently as I could until he was distracted in conversation with a group of soldiers. Then I went up to Johnny just as he was taking a canapé from a silver tray held up to him by a servant.

"Why, hello, Johnny." I tried to act as nonchalantly

as I could, despite the nervous beat of butterfly wings I felt within my stomach.

"Miss Tompkins!" he replied, doffing his cap. He took my hand and kissed it. I could not tell if he was genuinely happy to see me or just being perfunctorily polite. I looked back anxiously in Daddy's direction, but his back was still turned to me. Mama was in the kitchen with Mary. I turned again to Johnny and smiled as charmingly as I could. Maybe it was just the uniform, but he sure did look mighty handsome in it.

Then I asked, "Did you get my letter last summer before I went back to school? I gave it to Mary to bring ..."

"Yes, miss, I got it," he interrupted.

"Oh, good. And do call me Carlotta, please! I had hoped that you might write me back."

Now he slipped back into his old nervous stammer. He said, "I ... I meant to, Miss Tomp ... I mean Carlotta. But you see, I am not much of a writer, and well, I guess I didn't know what to say leastways, and ..."

"That is quite all right. But at least you know why I never came back to beat y'all at poker! I ..." At that moment, I heard a familiarly deep and booming voice behind me.

"Miss Carlotta?"

I turned to see Mary standing—looming rather—over me. She even made Johnny (now taller than the last time I had seen him) a dwarf by comparison. She looked anxious.

"Yes, Mary?"

"Your mama sent me to fetch you to the kitchen. And you best hurry too, 'cause I see your daddy fixin' his eye on you from over yonder!"

I glanced quickly again in Daddy's direction and, sure enough, he now stood alone, glaring at me from across the room. I looked back quickly at Johnny.

"Johnny, I ..."

"I understand," he nodded. "Take good care of yourself, Carlotta." He winked at me, which gave me an unexpected tingle of excitement.

"You too," said I. As I turned away, I added: "You write to me this time, Johnny, you hear?"

"Yes, ma'am!"

Johnny tipped his cap again as he turned back to join the other soldiers. Much would happen before we met again.

Mary was shaking her head at me.

"What now, Mary?

"You knows, Miss Carlotta. You knows!"

I later discovered that Daddy had recruited Johnny to join his regiment. Then I felt terrible at the thought of Johnny fighting and maybe getting hurt or even dying for people who could otherwise care less about him. I felt like it would be my fault if anything were to happen to him, and I thought about writing another letter to warn him. But soon afterward, when I looked out of my upstairs window one fine morning to watch Johnny marching away to war behind the Rebel flag to the sound of a drum and fife, I knew it was too late. He had made up his mind, and there was not a thing I could do to change it now. So, I just waved and hollered like everyone else lined up to watch them leave. As the soldiers passed beneath my window, I saw Johnny look up toward me and wink with a smile. I kept that image close to my heart from that day forward until I might see him again.

As the war progressed, things on the plantation went quickly from good to bad—and thence from there to worse. By the end of the year, Confederate strongholds in Kentucky had been overrun by Union troops one by one. Our plantation was no exception. But long before that, tragedy had already struck.

I anxiously hoped Johnny might write to me as promised this time. But when he did finally write later that summer, it was only to convey the worst news imaginable: Daddy had been shot and killed in Virginia at the First Battle of Bull Run on the twenty-first of July, the very first battle of the Civil War. Mama was beside herself with grief, especially after Daddy's body was finally returned home and she saw him buried.

Soon afterward, the Union army's blockade of Mississippi River ports in the South created hardship such as we had never imagined. Every simple commodity we always took for granted, from food to medicine and even basic items of clothing, became scarce.

When it became clear that it would not be long before Union soldiers came marching up to our very door to occupy our plantation, our relatives in town insisted that Mama send me away at once—as an attractive young lady going on eighteen and Daddy's only heir now to boot. We had old family friends (business associates of Daddy's) living up in Detroit, and everyone thought I should be sent there for safekeeping till the fighting ended. (Which everyone, of course, thought would be very soon indeed and most assuredly with a Confederate victory.) They also reckoned I could meet a nice gentleman there to marry—preferably a Southerner but at the very least Protestant and suitably rich, just as Daddy had wanted for me—whom I could bring back after the war to manage the plantation business I would inherit. Then we could all carry on as before with all the luxurious trappings of my accustomed wealth and privilege—supported, of course, by the continued free labor afforded by the many enslaved people we would still have at our command after winning the war. Much to my annoyance, Mama admitted her further motive of getting me as far away as possible from "that Jewish boy, in case he makes it back alive from the fighting."

Everything happened so quickly that I had little time to consider all these plans that others had now formed for me without so much as asking about my own desires. Besides, Mama was in such a state over Daddy's death that there was little point debating with her. She remained utterly inconsolable and could not be reasoned with. She wrote to our acquaintances in Detroit, and once the reply came back that I was welcome there, travel arrangements were quickly made. I was put on the next steamer upriver to Cincinnati, from there to take the train up to Toledo and from thence on to Detroit. Traveling with me, of course, was my ever-faithful nanny and servant (and, in my mind at least, my best friend), Mary Poindexter.

I was greeted at the railroad station by Mrs. Simms, an elderly widow originally from Lexington whose husband used to trade Daddy horses for the races. She lived alone with several paid servants in a large house near the train depot. One of her servants, a large colored man of about Mary's height, picked up our bags and escorted us to a small carriage waiting near the station, where another colored man in a similar uniform sat behind a lone horse, holding the reins in wait. This was the first time Mary had not been expected to handle all the luggage herself, and she stood watching awkwardly as the first servant loaded our bags (including her own) onto a rack beneath the carriage.

I supposed she knew full well that they were freemen actually being paid for their work, and that they knew, in turn, that she was enslaved. (Being from Kentucky early in the war could mean either, yet I supposed they guessed the truth right enough.) Then it occurred to me like a jolt that, here in Detroit, Mary could well resolve to up and run away, and there would be nothing I could do about it. I looked at her closely and decided this would be the test of whether she did indeed really care for me as a friend. For my part, I resolved right then and there that I would set her free whatever happened with the war. (This despite, I also decided, whatever any future husband might say.) Now that Daddy was dead, I figured I could make my own decisions. I still had much to learn about reality first.

I would pay Mary for her work, too, just as soon as I could afford it. But the scarcity of money was soon to be a problem I had never experienced or even imagined. At first, life in wartime Detroit was quite tolerable. Before leaving home, Mama had scrounged up all the available money left to us and given it to me for my expenses in Detroit. I only later discovered that she had given me just about all that was left of our family fortune and had little left to take care of herself and my sister, Ellie Mae. I still feel guilty to this day about the way I squandered most of it early on. The one thing I have always most feared in life ever since was being poor. Poor and alone.

Mrs. Simms was connected to the social elite in Detroit at that time and arranged for me to attend their functions designed to entertain—and marry off—the young. As the months flew by, I hardly noticed the passage of time while dancing the nights away almost every evening. But one night, while she was helping me dress, Mary met my eyes from behind my back in the mirror and gave me a stern look—that look of hers that always warned she was about to be square with me.

"Miss Carlotta," she began, "we been here almost three months now, and all you be doing is spend your Mama's money like it done growed on trees, ripe for the picking." I frowned and watched the mirror as Mary brushed my long, curly red locks. I always marveled at the reflection of her beautiful ebony-dark hands next to my pale white cheeks.

"You know," Mary continued, "you was sent here to get yourself a husband. Now you best find one befo' that money's all gone and you needs to find yourself a job instead. They be a lot of handsome young stallions out at them dances that would snap you right up. Ain't many gals like you around here that be both pretty as a pumpkin and got a big plantation!"

At that word "job," I froze. Mary knew right well that a young and genteel lady of my station would never wish to be caught dead doing an actual job. But she was right, frighteningly so: Mama had sent me there with the hope of securing a "suitable" husband who would take care of me till we could return home to the plantation after the war. Yet the idea of marrying for mere material convenience, without even a thought of the kind of true love and romance for which I had been longing ever since enacting the role of Juliet in school, seemed no better (and perhaps much worse) than the shameful grunt and sweat under a weary life of work. Leastways not while I was still awaiting the boy of my dreams to return. But there's the rub, and Mary read my thoughts.

She said, "Lawsy mercy, child! I hope you ain't still waiting for that good for nothin' Golden boy, neither. You knows what your mama would do if you brought him home."

I felt annoyed now. "And what would Mama do, Mary?"

"Why, she'd toss the both of you out with the dirty laundry, that's what. And me along with you! Now I know it ain't my place for to go preaching at you, Miss Carlotta. But you told me once to always tell it to you straight, and I declare to goodness that's what I is doing now. Tellin' it to you straight!"

I could not help but smile back at her in the mirror, but I could see from my reflection that it was a troubled smile beneath my freckled nose and dark brown eyes. I was troubled because I knew very well that Mary was right: that I now had some serious thinking to do about what to do next.

The answer came quite unexpectedly. An answer that proved the perfect compromise to buy time between getting a husband willy-nilly or having to seek a job before the war ended and I could return home. One day, Mrs. Simms introduced me to an older gentleman she said had been Daddy's good friend and business partner during his many visits to Detroit. Mr. Hopkins, it transpired, was a member of a prestigious gambling fraternity and used to take Daddy to his private club, where Daddy impressed the gentlemen there with his great skills at the poker table. Daddy had apparently bragged on me at some point to everyone there and told them about the spectacle I had made at casinos in New Orleans and Europe as a young girl prodigy at cards. So Mr. Hopkins invited me one day to the club, explaining that the members there had waived their strict "gentlemen only" rule to permit me to attend. (They would not, however, go so far as to allow Mary to join me.)

Well, needless to say, I made quite a splash there, and the men (mostly cigar-chomping, brandy-sipping elderly fellows) clearly did not mind getting fleeced of their money just for the pleasure of a few minutes' company with a charming young Southern belle. I quickly became a welcome fixture at the club, and with my daily winnings could support myself and Mary and even send money home to help Mama and Ellie Mae. Mama was now in ill-health, and she was worried about the cost of Ellie's education. The burden fell on my shoulders as the eldest child to support them in their hardship. Not wishing to bring shame to my family back home, I said nothing in my letters about where exactly the money came from. (Luckily, nobody asked).

That is also when I up and told Mary one day I was giving her an allowance—along with her freedom. When I arrived home one evening, I handed her a new purse filled with dollar bills.

"What's this, Miss Carlotta?"

"That's your new allowance, Mary. Along with a purse to keep it in!"

Mary reached into the purse and took out a few bills. She reacted like she had never held actual money before and gave me a perplexed look.

I said, "I suppose you know that you are free now!"

Mary appeared overwhelmed. "Free, Miss Carlotta?" I gave her a warm smile and touched her shoulder.

"That's right, Mary, free! We're up North now, after all, where slavery is illegal."

Mary looked at me like this must be some cruel joke. But after regarding me carefully for a moment, she suddenly burst into tears and hugged me so tightly I thought my back might break in two! Though I also felt something like I had never before felt start to well up inside me, I, too, broke into tears.

Mary abruptly let go and put down the purse, her expression somber.

She said, "You well knows what will happen to me and all my folk if the South wins this war. 'Specially if we go back to your plantation."

"Not in my book! Anyway, if I say you're free, then that is how it will be. Anybody who works for me will be paid for their labor, whatever they might say back home."

Mary gave me a dubious look.

"Including," I reassured her, "any future husband of mine!" I picked up the purse and handed it back to Mary. "Please, I insist."

Mary hesitated again but then accepted the purse with a gracious smile. After that, I understood very clearly for the first time the utter, inhuman, and downright evil cruelty of slavery and resolved to do all I could to fight it, whoever won the war.

After nearly a year of my daily routine at the club, I grew tired of spending day after day in a dimly lit, smoke-filled room among such stodgy old men and longed for a sea change. It was right around then, in September of 1862, that Johnny turned up.

Once he arrived, it did not take long to learn the whereabouts of a young Kentucky belle and her giant Negro nanny. Unfortunately, my having never told him of my parents' true feelings about him meant he did not hesitate to come directly to our door without discretion, and little did I likewise know that Mama had told Mrs. Simms all about Johnny and asked her to be on the watch for him.

I was over the moon to see him, of course. I had often daydreamed again on cold Detroit days about those summer afternoons at the track in Kentucky playing cards and grooming horses with Johnny. Now, he stood on the front porch, staring at me.

"Miss Carlotta," he smiled.

"Just Carlotta, please!" I took his arm, and we walked to the riverfront street beyond the house. I glanced back to see Mary shaking her head disapprovingly in the doorway and noticed Mrs. Simms watching intently from the window. A shadow of doubt cast a momentary pall over my heart, but it quickly passed as I led Johnny along the busy avenue crowded with horses, many of them pulling carriages and just as many bearing men—including Union soldiers—on horseback. Johnny wore a plain flannel shirt, and I wondered what he had done with his Confederate uniform. It would not do at all for him to be caught with it up North at that time! But I figured he knew better than to reveal his true loyalties anywhere north of the Mason-Dixon line. There were many Southern sympathizers there, it was true, especially with all of the river traffic, but opinions were so divided (especially on the matter of slavery) that most people—in the early days of the war, at least—shied away from discussing politics lest anyone be offended. One often did not know on which side even one's closest family members' true sympathies lay, and people had begun to dread family gatherings such as Thanksgiving and Christmas.

As we walked arm in arm along the river quay, I was eager to hear his news and anything he could tell me of home.

I asked, "But how are you here?"

"When I got your letter, I resolved to come see you as soon as I got leave."

A battalion of blue-uniformed Union Soldiers

marched past, and Johnny picked up his pace nervously. I looked at him concerned.

"I hope your own uniform is hidden well out of sight up here!"

Johnny nodded with a nervous smile. "I only have a few days. We've been hard-pressed to hold back General Grant's troops and a complete Union occupation of Kentucky." Seeing my look of concern, he added: "Don't worry. Your mother and sister were fine when I left. They're still safe for now, and I'll see to it personally that they remain so!"

Despite his reassuring smile, I felt doubtful.

"Thank you, Johnny..."

Seeing my anxious look, he added: "I'd be lying if I told you everything was grand there. With your father dead, most of the servants have fled, and there's nobody left to plant the crops."

"I feared as much."

"And then ... there's your mother's health."

This naturally alarmed me. "What of it?"

"When I left, she was very ill."

I felt devastated at this news, but after a moment regained my composure.

"Tell me about the fighting down South. Have you seen much of it?"

Johnny's face suddenly blanched with a look of terror such as I had never seen in a man. Something about his demeanor seemed to transform in a way that wholly unsettled me at that moment.

"If you could only imagine what I have seen ..." His voice trailed off, and he looked across the river as if there were something on the other side that only he could see. I moved in closer to him and instinctively took his hand.

I said, "What do you see when you look over yonder?"

He did not answer. I followed his eyes and stared across the Detroit River at the vast Canadian landscape beyond. We stood that way in silence for some time before he turned and looked deeply into my eyes. He seemed like a wholly different person than I had known back home. No longer just a young boy of fifteen, but a boy who had been thrust into manhood before his time and shown things about life and death and terrible human suffering that had already changed him irreparably. I could not know it then, but he must have been suffering from what they now call (after the horrors of similar trench warfare in the recent Great War), "shell shock." I could not even imagine what he had been through and seen in battle.

But something about the pain in Johnny's eyes that day by the river drew me closer to him, and before I knew it, our lips were touching. It was my first kiss. Judging from Johnny's awkwardness then and especially during what happened afterward, I felt sure it must have been his first, too. We walked in silence aimlessly for a while, until a sudden notion struck me. I had never before experienced such intense feelings (both emotionally and physically) as I felt while kissing Johnny, but I knew this was what it meant to really want somebody. I had often read about it in books, but now it was suddenly real. I abruptly stopped and drew him into another embrace.

I asked softly, "Where are you staying?"

Johnny hesitated a moment, then shyly pointed his chin ahead of us.

"That hotel up yonder." I nodded, retook his arm, and turned us in that direction. That day is one I will never forget.

When we got to his room, the first thing Johnny did was close the curtains. When he turned around, he saw me standing motionless before him, my expression no doubt some combination of both innocence and seductive expectation. He stepped toward me, and we fell at once into a passionate kiss and proceeded to rip off each other's clothing. Then we fell onto the bed and made love with abandon.

3

LATER THAT DAY, as we walked arm in arm by the river at sunset, I decided to tell Johnny what my parents—especially my father—had said about him. To my surprise, he nodded his head as if he already knew.

"But why is that?" I asked. "What do my people have against the Jews?"

Johnny looked down for a moment before answering. Then he said, "It has always been that way. Throughout our history."

"But why? Is it only because of religion?"

"Partly, I guess. But it goes much further back than

that. My people have often been looked at as outsiders. Wherever we've gone throughout our history, we have always been perceived as a threat."

"Why a threat?"

"We Jews are a very industrious people, Carlotta. We work hard and tend to succeed in whatever business we set our hearts and minds to. That makes other people jealous and suspicious of us. So they call us cruel names—and sometimes much worse."

I drew him closer to me but said nothing, as I could tell he was deep in thought and preparing to share more.

"People often use religion," he continued, "to justify their hatred. They blame all of society's problems on the Jews to avoid admitting their own faults. Even now, this whole war and the shattered economy it's caused is getting blamed on us by people from both sides!"

I asked, "But why are you fighting for the South?"

Johnny laughed sardonically to himself. "Just trying to fit in where I happened to be, I guess. It hardly matters, anyway. I hear General Ulysses Grant is planning to expel all Jews from the districts he commands, including in Kentucky. Even if I wanted to switch sides and fight for the North, they'd kick me out anyway! So you see, it hardly matters what side I fight for, 'cause nobody's really on my side!" He shrugged and then smiled at me. "That's why Jewish families like mine are so protective of one another. And suspicious of you gentiles!"

"What will your family in Boston think of me?"

"My parents will be furious, of course. Especially my mother!"

I felt tears welling up in my eyes. I was struggling to find any words in response when Johnny took my hand and said something completely unexpected.

"Marry me, Carlotta!"

"Marry you? But..."

"But me no buts, as my mother likes to say. I love you, Carlotta! Let's get married just as soon as this hellish war is done. Then we can leave everything behind!"

"Where will we go?"

"We'll head West! That's the future, where all opportunity now lies. And between the two of us working as a team, we can gamble our way to California and strike it rich there in gold! Well, what do you say?"

He looked at me with such an eagerness in his eyes that I noticed it seemed to have replaced the pain that had been there before. As confused as I felt about his sudden proposition, I did not have the heart to disappoint him. So I decided to acquiesce, at least for now, and gave him a timid nod of affirmation.

Johnny continued: "There's no point in returning home any time soon anyway. I fear your plantation will be occupied by Union soldiers by the time I get back. But don't worry, I am sure your mother and sister will be safe despite it all. It would be best if you boarded a steamer down the Mississippi as soon as you can. With your gambling skills, you can make a fortune by the time you reach New Orleans. From there, you can win enough money to get to San Antonio, and that's where I shall meet you when I'm discharged. The war should be over by then, and we can travel west together from there!"

Without thinking further about it, I consented. In

my naïveté, this seemed too exciting a proposition to pass up.

"All right, Johnny. I will!"

"Take Mary with you," Johnny added. "She'll protect you along the way."

We embraced again, and I felt another sharp pang of doubt. But I managed a laugh and answered: "But of course!"

That is how I came to leave Detroit and everything that was expected of me there, and soon headed off with Mary on a new and uncertain adventure. I had made up my mind. I would head to Texas.

I bade farewell to Johnny that next morning at the train depot, complete with a passionate farewell kiss of which I am often reminded now at the new "talkies" on the silver screen.

"See you in Texas, Carlotta!" he shouted as he boarded the train. "I'll find you in the Alamo City!"

"See you in Texas," I mumbled in reply. Already, I was having doubts. Not so much about the intriguing idea of heading west (and its clear dangers), but about Johnny. There was something about him that did not feel right inside somehow. Something connected to the pain and a certain "disconnectedness" I had continued to observe in his eyes and behavior since his arrival and our brief but passionate time together. Yet I managed to bury these concerns for now and began planning my trip downriver over the coming weeks, while continuing to save up my poker winnings from the club to fund the passage south for myself and Mary.

It is funny now to recall how I saw gambling then as just a temporary measure to get me through until I could return home and resume my role as an heiress and head of the plantation—along with all the fancy trappings that accompanied such a wealthy and privileged lifestyle. Up till now, my destiny in life—at least the one planned for me by my parents and my particular station in society—was to have married a rich gentleman from a good local Southern family who would help me manage the plantation: a plantation that would continue to prosper indefinitely (enslaved people and all) through our progeny for generations to come. But none of this seemed now meant to be. I had a clear choice: to return home penniless and disgraced (no doubt word of my gambling—and Johnny—would precede me) and live out my days in misery and destitution, or I could take my chances and, like so many lost souls at that time, set out West in search of good fortune in both riches and (in my case at least) love and happiness. I chose the latter option, but nothing could ever have prepared me for where I would ultimately be led—and what I would find there.

It was a desperate plan, but I was desperate now, too, and saw this as my only remaining choice. I wanted it all—independence and happiness—in a world where women rarely found either. I missed Mama and Ellie Mae terribly, and often (especially when I felt lonely), I wished I could go back home to them. But something also told me I would see neither home nor them ever again.

In the meantime, I received a letter from my sister chock-full of bad news. As I sat at the mirror in my boudoir, reading it in distress, Mary watched me with concern.

She asked, "From your sister?"

I nodded. "She says Mama's had a stroke! She's near paralyzed from head to foot and laid up in bed for good."

Mary touched my shoulder to comfort me. "I'm sorry, Miss Carlotta!"

"That's not all, Mary ..." I lowered my voice and looked toward the door. "Mrs. Simms wrote and told Mama about Johnny visiting here. Ellie Mae says Mama's furious and plans to disown me if I marry him!"

"Sakes alive! But you can't say I didn't warn you about that boy, now, Miss Carlotta!"

I angrily tore up the letter. "I know you did, but it's my business whom I choose to be with." I stared at Mary, who nodded empathetically.

"But what you gonna do now?"

I gave her a look of resolve. "What we are going to do is head south!"

Mary looked worried. "South?"

"Don't worry, Mary! We're going all the way down to New Orleans. It's under Union occupation now, along with most of the river south. You'll be safe and free, and we can ride out the war there."

"New Orleans? Goodness gracious me! But how are we going to get there?"

I smiled. "Just leave that to me, Mary!"

So, just as Mary had predicted, Mama threatened to disown me if I were to marry Johnny or even to further associate with him (not to mention ever bringing him home). Not that it mattered, what with all the family money just about gone anyhow, and seeing as the plantation appeared doomed to Union occupation any day now. But the sting of Mama's words still hurt me deeply, just as those of Daddy had done before the war that summer when all had seemed so magical with Johnny.

Indeed, I often still found myself dreaming of those lost summers on the plantation—when my only occupation was lying in the cool green grass by the pond, listening to the wind singing in the leaves of overhanging trees, and the whirring hum of cicadas that Mama called katydids. Now, it was up to me to fend entirely for myself while still supporting my family back home. I resolved to find a way to keep both my ailing mother and my sister, along with providing for Ellie Mae's increasingly essential education if she were to live a respectable life as a lady in Kentucky.

Unfortunately, my sister also informed me that Mama demanded to know the source of the money I was sending home. She had heard rumors, and I knew before long the gossip might quickly devolve into that of a most unsavory kind. Despite the disgrace this would bring to my family, it also meant they might refuse my help even despite its urgency. So, I concocted a little story that I hoped would dispel doubts and allow me to continue sending money home without a hint of scandal.

I wrote back to tell them that Johnny had left for good and that I had now met a wealthy gentleman in

Detroit who wanted to marry me and take me to his home in Texas, where he had made his fortune as a cattleman. He had very kindly offered to provide money both to support Mama and to pay for Ellie Mae's education. I wrote that we would soon be departing by steamboat downriver to New Orleans, where we would visit that fine city for a spell before heading west to my new husband's home in San Antonio. (I also knew New Orleans was now under Union control and should be a safe place for Mary and me to ride out the war.) This would explain both my time in New Orleans and my eventual journey to Texas. I instructed my sister to apprise me of Mama's condition by telegraph that I could receive at the New Orleans Western Union office. I hated fabricating such a lie to cover for myself, and I felt mighty guilty about it. But I justified it to myself with the rationalization that I had no choice but to do so. It would not be the last such rationalization that I would be forced to make for myself upon bending the truth a little. However, I found it did get easier with practice.

Likewise, I told Mrs. Simms that I was leaving for New Orleans with Mary to undertake urgent family business. I knew such a notion must seem far-fetched, especially for a young lady traveling alone (during wartime, at that). I just hoped I could rely on her elderly gullibility to prevent Mrs. Simms from writing to Mama and contradicting my "rich Texas rancher" story that she could easily debunk.

I finally booked passage for myself and Mary on a shiny new paddle wheel, triple-deck sternwheeler christened the New Orleans (after Robert Fulton's first commercial steamboat fifty years earlier). I traveled to Pittsburgh with Mary, where the New Orleans was docked on schedule. From there, the paddle steamer would head south down the Ohio River until reaching the Mississippi at Cairo, Illinois, and thence downriver through Memphis and Natchez and finally to New Orleans after an almost three-month voyage of over eighteen hundred miles.

One cold but sunny morning in early spring 1863, I found myself starting up the boarding gangplank with Mary. We must have been some sight, too: a petite nineteen-year-old girl with flaming red sunlit locks climbing the platform with an ebony giant of a woman by my side and lugging our own respective baggage, too!

4

I KNEW OUR ROUTE would take us past Warsaw, Kentucky, and that we would probably stop there, so I would have to be careful to stay hidden to avoid being spotted. This was made easier on account of the women passengers being separated from the men for the most part and confined to second-class "deck passage"—along with immigrants and servants.

I had other plans, however: I had spotted an elderly gentleman whom I recognized from the poker club in Detroit and—in hopes of an invite to a private saloon in the upper deck—formed a plan to ingratiate myself to him at the first opportunity. Women were, of course, generally kept as far as possible from bars, following the outrageous notion that ladies and liquor should never mix company. Despite such chauvinistic policies, my little scheme worked brilliantly, and for the remainder of the trip, I worked the poker table to both the delight—and the increasing dismay—of the gentlemen passengers as the lone lady gambler in their midst.

Not all were *gentlemen,* mind you: There were ruffians aplenty aboard our ship, too, some of them professional gamblers who made their livings preying on affluent yet naïve passengers. It was the professional riverboat gambler you had to watch out for. They were as mean and crude and as dirty at cards as they come, and all they ever did was cheat. I tried my best to avoid these, as their wary eyes could easily spot the most subtle sleights of hand that Daddy had taught me. (Fortunately, thanks also to Daddy, I knew most of their tricks too.) I set my sights instead on the many young and chivalrous gentlemen on board. I learned to use my wiles to charm them into a round of poker, only to fleece those innocent pigeons for all they had.

In this way, we made our progress slowly south, with me raking in cash at the tables while Mary waited patiently below decks for me to return and take her along for my afternoon perambulations above decks and—when docked—at the various landings along the way. (I would never stroll alone without Mary, especially having observed more than one sinister-eyed ruffian follow my movements with a certain lusty malice, but one look in turn from Mary's evil eye could intimidate the devil himself.) Despite our ship being Union-controlled, Mary was forced to stay on the lower decks unless escorted by me. But between us, she knew that–in my mind–she was now free as a bird and that it was just a question of biding our time until I no longer had to play the ruse of being a Southern slave heiress. Yet, with the palpable tension on board among fellow passengers from both North and South, we knew we had best play our expected roles for now.

A few days past a brief stop in Cincinnati, I saw the familiar old landing at Warsaw. We stayed discreetly below decks in our cabin till, at the piercing whine of a loud whistle, we felt the jolt of the giant paddle wheel relaunch our ship with a sudden roar of steam power. I watched anxiously through a porthole window to see if anyone I recognized boarded there. Nobody did, but what I did see were troops of soldiers in dark blue patrolling along the dock. Clearly, Warsaw was now under Federal occupation, and I shuddered to think what might be happening back home on the plantation. I could only pray for them and hope to have news from Ellie Mae upon arrival in New Orleans.

As I learned later, this was also the reason for our safe passage downriver. By that time, Union forces generally patrolled the rivers, with garrisons at the various ports and gunboats controlling river traffic to protect goods being transported North. And so our vessel trudged its steady ten miles per hour pace downstream, a relatively uneventful journey once we got past the roaring rapids at the treacherous Falls of the Ohio just past Louisville. There—at the same place where Lewis and Clark had once met up in 1803 to plan that famous little expedition of their own—the Ohio River drops twenty-six feet in the course of a mile over a rise of limestone bedrock. At one point, our hardy captain feared the water might be too low to proceed. But once he and his crew had navigated us safely through, we continued apace until finally meeting the mighty Mississippi where the Ohio converges with it just south of Cairo, Illinois. At that point, the brown, sediment-laden water of the Ohio flows into the greenish water of the Mississippi River. Also green were the distant riverbanks, where luscious pine forests bounded us on both sides. Looking out at this beautiful scenery, I hummed an old folk ballad I had heard once in the Appalachians.

Now darlin,' my darlin'
Don't tell me no lie,
Tell me, where did you stay last night?

In the pines, in the pines
Where the sun never shines,
I shivered when the cold wind blowed.

There, where the landscape suddenly opened up gloriously on both sides of the vast river, I first felt an invigorating sense of genuine freedom. I loved to stand in the open air of the foredeck in the shadow of the pilot house, Mary by my side, and inhale the perfume of flowers lining the rails—pungent gardenia and sweet azalea blossoms. A frantic whir of tiny hummingbird wings made a pleasant change from the accustomed whine of mosquitoes and gnats. Nights were especially magical, the way the dark roiling water behind our ship's paddle glinted moonlight in its foam. In the darkness across the river, glow-worms big as lanterns illumined the night. Nothing compared to looking up at the night sky, where on clear nights, the stars appeared like a billion pinpricks in some cosmic blanket through which the light of Heaven beyond drew enchanted constellations.

On such nights, the sultry, humid summer air was often pierced with music when the joyful banter of banjos and mandolins on deck would sometimes compete for our attention with the more sonorous melodies of the saloon piano. But it was not always such clear sailing. Sometimes, a summer storm would announce itself with a sudden clap of thunder, followed by the swift patter of rain on the water below, from which steam would rise up as if the river were on fire. But when lightning began to strike, and the clouds emptied their giant buckets upon us in torrential rain, Mary and I hightailed it below deck rather than putting too much stock in Ben Franklin's lightning rods adorning the ship!

When we reached Memphis, our captain had a new concern. This part of the Mississippi was notoriously dangerous for steamboats such as ours, ever since the New Madrid earthquake of 1811 had devastated the region and raised many perilous snags along the banks. With their twisted branches and roots, these sunken trees could lurk unseen beneath the water and impale passing ships with deadly consequences. (Such a fate had indeed befallen our ship's namesake; a hidden snag had sunk the first New Orleans steamship in 1814.) However, the savvy captain carefully navigated through the marked shallows whilst still managing to dock at the Memphis port.

The Federals had occupied this highly strategic river gateway–once among the South's largest cotton (and slave) markets–since defeating the Confederates in the naval battle of '62, so Mary and I were able safely to disembark for a much-desired respite on dry land. While there, I managed to join a small group of Union soldiers I spotted playing poker outside near the ship. One of them clearly took a shine to me, too–until, that is, I had shone him up at cards and emptied his wallet. The parting look he shot at me might have warned me to watch out for him downriver, especially after overhearing that the men were part of a cavalry regiment heading south to New Orleans themselves. But I still had much to learn about sore losers (especially when they were insecure men losing to women!). In the meantime, our next visit to shore was very nearly tragic.

The river grew ever wider as we journeyed southward, often past large islands midstream. When we reached the confluence of the Mississippi and Arkansas rivers, there was a landing on the Arkansas Delta. The riverport town there was called Napoleon, and it was there that we stopped again.

I read long afterward how that town would soon suffer a disastrous fate. After the occupying Union troops dug a channel through the narrow land separating the Mississippi and Arkansas upriver to aid their gunboats, the town of Napoleon would eventually be entirely submerged by river floodwaters. Mark Twain later wrote about it in one of my favorite books, his *Life on the Mississippi,* where he described the ghostly image of floating over the town he once knew and loved:

Yes, it was an astonishing thing to see the Mississippi rolling between unpeopled shores and straight over the spot where I used to see a good big self-complacent town twenty years ago ... a city no more—swallowed up, vanished, gone to feed the fishes; nothing left but a fragment of a shanty and a crumbling brick chimney!

Yet for us that day, Napoleon was still a thriving, bustling community. It was also where Mary and I both had a near-fatal fright.

The Captain informed us that our stay would be brief—just long enough to load some much-needed supplies and fuel for the boilers—but that passengers could have the afternoon to stroll about the town. I walked along the bank rather briskly, my colorful parasol in hand, until I was ahead of Mary a piece despite her long stride. Suddenly, I heard her shout from behind in her deep voice, almost a scream even. She yelled, "Stop, Miss Carlotta! Watch your step!"

I saw a giant water moccasin snake on the bank right before me. I screamed, but before I knew what hit me, I was flung to the ground with one sweep of Mary's strong arm. I looked up just in time to see a long shape with numerous dark bands attached to Mary's hand. It was the largest such pit viper I had ever seen. It was sunning itself on the bank when I nearly stepped on it, but Mary saw it first, and—after pushing me aside—threw herself upon the serpent right before it struck. The snake now dangled from her hand as she tried to free herself from the grasp of its sharp fangs. The cat-like pupils seemed to glare at her hatefully, and I knew she would now consider herself forever cursed and under the "snake-eye" spell.

The snake finally let go after she pinned its writhing body to the ground with her foot. She then quickly grasped a sharp-edged rock near at hand and smashed the diamond-shaped head before tossing the now limp, scaly body far out into the river. Despite the pain in her hand, the first thing Mary did was rush over to my side. At that moment, I felt a new sense of deep devotion toward Mary as a loyal friend. And I knew she may have just saved my life at the risk of her own.

"You all right, Miss Carlotta?"

"I'm fine, thank you Mary. But look at your hand; you must see the ship's doctor at once!"

For the next few days, Mary lay in her bed below deck suffering from a high fever and hallucinations. Fortunately for her, the on-board doctor was something of an expert in treating snake bites—particularly those of the river variety, having seen his share as a ship's doctor—and he had responded to my urgent pleas by attending to her promptly.

He said, "She'll have to lose her little finger to keep the venom from spreading. But if she recovers from the fever, she might still live."

"Might? I don't like the sound of that! How long

before we know, doctor?"

"She will likely be bedridden till we reach New Orleans. But, with luck, she will make a full recovery."

"With luck?"

I remained, for the most part, with Mary in our quarters for some time afterward, tending to her wound and praying for her recovery—though I did venture up to the deck occasionally to observe the sights. As we drifted further south, the years of recent warfare were all the more evident. There were many burnt and empty fields along both sides of the river, where the cotton and other crops had been abandoned to rot. There were recent battlefields, such as Vicksburg, where the muddy trenches appeared still stained with blood, lined with hundreds upon hundreds of temporary graves with small wooden crosses. Sometimes, I could see empty plantation houses in the distance. Some were still quite beautiful, but others had been burned to the ground, with occasional chimneys, Greek revival pedestals, and columns standing like ancient ruins from some distant land. These images brought back my worries about our plantation in Kentucky. At such times, I would grasp the rails tightly and silently pray for my mother and sister, anxious for news from home.

At Natchez, many beautiful estates along the river had survived. There, the Confederates surrendered early in the war without a fight soon after the fall of New Orleans, and many of the old mansions were now occupied by Union troops. (General Grant himself occupied the famous Rosalie Mansion as his headquarters in

1863.)

Soon after passing through Natchez, Mary made a miraculous recovery and was soon on her feet again, joining me on deck to view the changing landscape. If her bandaged hand troubled her, she stoically ignored it. The only pain she showed was from within, as I could see in her eyes when we passed numerous refugee camps where thousands of formerly enslaved people struggled to survive in destitute living conditions. President Lincoln first issued the Emancipation Proclamation in '62, and it took effect on the first of January 1863. Federal troops were now busy closing down slave markets and liberating captives from the horrors of human slavery at each city they captured; yet while the war still raged, they were largely still confined to these sordid camps. Many of the freedmen eagerly joined in the fighting against their former masters and were organized into separate regiments of their own. Whenever I looked at Mary now, I felt an ever-deepening sense of guilt for having been raised in a so-called "civilized" society that could condone such monstrous barbarity.

As we journeyed on down into Louisiana, we also saw occasional bands of Indians—men, women, and children—watching us from the river banks, their eyes filled with a depth of sadness such as I had never seen. We sometimes saw their campfires glowing red through the woods at night. The still evening air was often punctuated with a solemn drumbeat, and the melancholy cadence of their sacred chants drifted across the moonlit water.

They, too, were displaced, mostly remnants of

Choctaw and Cherokee tribes forcibly removed during the shameful Trail of Tears travesty, perpetrated by President Andrew Jackson and continued as hostile policy toward our native peoples by Van Buren and subsequent presidents. It was only later (after I finally reached the Texas frontier in the midst of the Texas-Indian wars) that I fully understood the true nature of their struggle to keep their ancestral lands and way of life.

Baton Rouge was our last major stop before the long sternwheeler journey finally approached its conclusion at New Orleans. The landscape changed drastically as we ventured deeper south into the swampy regions of Louisiana. One misty morning, as Mary and I stood on the stern of the Texas deck enjoying a cool breeze infused with the sweet scent of wild honeysuckle and wisteria blooming along the bank, a large dark shape surfaced in the water just below us. As I peered over the railing for a closer look, I jumped back, startled to see a pair of sinister-looking yellow eyes staring back at me. Just then, a young man with eyes even darker than mine stepped up beside me and said in a thick Cajun drawl: "Don't let them gators get y'all!" He pointed toward the bank, where we could see through the clearing fog several more enormous alligators lying in the sand.

"My heavens!" I smiled at the fellow and lightly touched his arm. "I don't recall ever seeing such critters back home in Kentucky."

He said, "You ain't in Kentucky no more, lady." Then he winked at me before sauntering off toward the gambling parlor, and Mary glanced at me with a knowing smile. I had just gained a gullible new customer for my card table.

That's where the "sore loser" I mentioned earlier comes in, when I learned the hard way about the perils of playing too many of Daddy's old tricks at once for the sake of winning at all costs. Our steamboat finally docked at the landing in New Orleans, and we had just stepped off the boarding ramp with our luggage when I heard a voice behind me, this time an angry shout.

"Hey, lady! Hold it right there, you cheatin' little whore!"

I turned around to see the Union soldier from Memphis who had frightened me with his appearance. He was pointing at me while speaking angrily to a group of soldiers.

I tried to remain calm while looking around for a means of escape. There was none. Soldiers quickly surrounded us, and they were all now staring at me with looks of hostile intent.

PART II

The Angel of San Antonio

5

SEVERAL THINGS NOW HAPPENED at once. First, the piercing whine of our steamer's whistle sounded above the deck from where we had just descended. I attempted to step backward onto the plank and head back up, hoping to find safety aboard ship. But the way was shut off by a wooden gate now that all passengers had disembarked. I looked frantically for possible help but saw naught but distant stevedores busily unloading cargo. At that moment, the soldier lunged forward with the most frightening look I had ever seen.

"I finally figured out how you done it!" he shouted as he strode toward me. "You was dealin' dirty from the bottom of your deck. That's how you stole all my money. And now I aim to whip you good for it!" He reached out to grab me, but suddenly Mary leapt into his way and stood firm, towering before him like some Amazonian warrior.

Mary shouted, "No, you ain't, mistah!"

She grabbed the young man with her good hand

and dragged him with her powerful arm onto the dock. Before he even knew what had hit him, Mary threw him out into the river's muddy waters, just as she had done with that snake up in Arkansas.

I looked back with dread at the other soldiers surrounding us, fearing their angry retribution. But to my great relief, they were all laughing hilariously. One of them shouted, "Let's get a drink!" At that, they all quickly departed in a rush to the taverns of New Orleans. I sighed with a deep breath and turned back to Mary. She was still keeping an intent watch on the soldier as he floundered in the river before finally stumbling around on land sopping-wet in his blue uniform. He took one look at us and hastened off in the opposite direction. We never saw him again.

The first thing I did was to find the Western Union telegraph office. There, as I had both hoped and dreaded, a telegram awaited me from my sister. I opened it apprehensively, and for good reason. It was just as I feared: Mama had died.

Though I had anticipated my mother's death, it was devastating all the same. We had often had our differences, to be sure, my mother and me. But the sudden realization that she was no longer in the world and that I would never see her again was soul-wrenching. At least with Daddy, I got to see him again when his body was returned for burial, and I was there for his funeral.

Now, I was a long, long way from home with little prospect of ever returning, and both of my parents were gone. All I had left was my sister Ellie Mae, and I did not figure on seeing her again anytime soon either (if ever at all). But I reckoned I owed something to her as her older sister and for our parents' memory. So I resolved to fulfill my duty of ensuring she finished her education and could maintain her social standing to whatever extent possible after the war and its likely outcome for plantations such as ours. As I also learned from Ellie's telegram, our plantation was now under the control of Union troops, who occupied both it and the port town of Warsaw. The safest place for her now was her boarding school, after which she would soon come of age and–I hoped–find a husband to take good care of her. (A rather hypocritical hope on my part–but given her age and location and the current circumstances there, it was truly her best option: first and foremost for security and then, with luck, some degree of happiness too.)

Though I did not wish to admit it, my mother's passing nevertheless lightened my financial burden significantly. Now, apart from Mary and myself, I had only to earn enough money to support my sister. Otherwise, my priority was to save up enough for the trip to Texas.

All told, we spent almost two years in New Orleans, while the war ravaged on in the world outside. But until it finally ended, little changed in the "good time city" (as Daddy always called the Crescent City). The place still possessed its Old World charms, especially as a center of the latest European–and especially French–culture and haute couture fashion. (In none of which could I fully partake, given my meager purse and obligation to save.)

However, wartime New Orleans also possessed a certain worn-down feeling, an almost palpable aura of fatigue. It lacked the elegant and exuberant luster I so fondly recalled from my childhood visits with Daddy, which gave it, in turn, a touch of ineffable melancholy despite the surface frivolity.

After reacquainting myself with some of Daddy's old Thoroughbred racing business (and gambling) partners there, I found a warm welcome in the city's most prestigious gambling halls, soon becoming the talk of the town as both Daddy's protégé and as a formidable "lady gambler" in my own right. Famous casinos and drinking houses in "the Swamp," like those at the St. Charles Hotel and on the local riverboats, became my regular stomping ground.

In my free hours, I frequented the old French Quarter with its exquisite cafes, including Antoine's Restaurant, Tujague's, and *Café Du Monde* with their scrumptious *beignets*. My favorite place was a café on Bourbon Street called *La Rose Fanée*, where I discovered the delights of the local cuisine. After a long night of flipping cards, nothing warmed the palate like a large bowl of spicy red beans and rice, or a plate of their plumb delicious "Shrimp Tchoupitoulas"–juicy shrimp sauteed with mushrooms and soaked in a tangy garlic sauce (often enjoyed to the quick-tempo accordion sounds of Cajun Zydeco music). My favorites, though, were the crawfish *étouffée* and shrimp Creole, and I even acquired a Creole cookbook to savor these delicacies wherever my road should take me. Mary and I were both fascinated with the French Creole culture, though I quickly found the French I had learned as a girl on trips to Europe with Daddy sounded flat next to the spicy dialect of the Louisiana locals.

At *La Rose Fanée,* an old regular used to sit at the bar telling tales. His name was Charlie, but his friends called him "Buddy." He had come down to Texas from Arkansas to volunteer in the Mexican War and eventually wound up in New Orleans. From Buddy, I learned a lot of history (though how true it was, I never knew) about the Texas and Arkansas frontier. His vivid descriptions of the gritty characters and landscape there filled me with a desire to see it all for myself!

Yet it was when he spoke of his experiences in the Mexican War that Buddy waxed especially emotional. One evening, he told the story of a time when he and a fellow soldier became separated from the company of Texas Rangers in which they were serving. They hiked along the Rio Grande near Laredo and came across an abandoned village in which the only structure still standing amidst a wasteland of smoldering rubble was an old Spanish mission. Upon the plaza before it lay countless bodies, many of them women and children, and the two men were sickened by the smell of rotting flesh.

Buddy and his comrade sought shelter in the mission and spent a restless night amongst the stench and the tumult of distant battle. The next morning, as they stepped warily outside and prepared to resume the search for their company, there was a blast of nearby cannon fire followed by an explosion just behind them. They instinctively fell to the ground and covered their heads. When they looked up again, they saw that the church from which they had just emerged was now but a smoking pile of rubble.

At that, Buddy abruptly ceased his tale and went silent. He would say no more that night, and he seldom spoke of his war experiences again.

Despite the city's Federal occupation, Mary was not allowed to enter any of these places with me. She nonetheless expressed significant relief at the contrast from our earlier visits before the war, when the port was filled with the ungodly sight of slave pens and human auctions, and when she was under the close watch of Daddy—for whom she was nothing more than a material possession and a useful tool. Back then, an enslaved person caught after the sun went down could be publicly whipped. Now she was at some liberty, although it was understood between us that—in public at least—we must retain the old ruse (especially in front of Daddy's former associates on whom my access to the casinos, and hence our very welfare, depended).

In time, I grew restless, bored, and ready to move on. My coffers were full, and I had a trunk full of fine Parisian fashion, too. Yet the war's end ultimately dictated our move to Texas. It was soon after the Mardi Gras parade of '65—the first Mardi Gras festivities held in New Orleans since the war began, and therefore especially extravagant and festive with the return of the "Mistick Krewe of Comus" that year—that word came the war had finally ended on April 9, 1865 (almost four years to the day since it started). New Orleans erupted in joy at that good news—a celebration that might have continued indefinitely, were it not for the sobering news later that week of President Lincoln's assassination.

A month after celebrating my twenty-first birthday, Mary and I finally found ourselves on a stage-coach heading West toward San Antonio in late May of that year. I had heard nothing from Johnny in all that time and knew not if I might find him there—though I also knew he was most likely killed in the war.

Little could I guess what a grand—if often down-right perilous—adventure now lay before me. Yet, whether good or bad, I knew I must ultimately embrace my fate.

6

SO READ THE SIGN, in the shape of a hand pointing west, along the dusty road leading to the Sabine River ferry. A thriving town was built up there by the old Gaine's ferry, an important shipping point for cotton and other goods awaiting steamboat transport to the prairie lands of northeast Texas. The muddy river banks were lined with warehouses.

The old sign at the entrance still read "12 ½ Cents for a Person or a Horse," even though the half-penny had been abolished before the war and replaced in 1864 with a two-cent coin—with the new motto "In God We Trust" emblazoned on the front over the Great Seal. (The three-cent nickel had just been approved by President Lincoln a month before his assassination and was not yet in circulation, while the five-cent nickel was still another year away.) So the ferryman demanded thirteen pennies apiece for Mary and me, which I carefully counted out from my coin purse that Mary kept safely in her top outercoat pocket. I handed them to the ferryman, who immediately commenced a careful recount despite having already scrutinized every coin as it was placed individually into his outstretched palm. As he stared at me with bulbous eyes protruding from his almost ghostly pale face, I fancied he was Charon ferrying souls across the Styx into Hades beyond.

Once all had boarded the ferry, we began our slow progress across the river. It was still early, and the further bank was shrouded in fog, but through shreds of mist, there were glimpses of the flat landscape beyond. As the Texas riverbank came gradually closer, I felt anew the thrill of the unknown adventure ahead. I reflected on all that had led to this moment in my life, and all the unknowns that lay ahead. Where would my destiny lead? Who would I meet? Would I even long survive the perils of this notoriously rough-and-tumble land? Time only would tell.

For now, as we drifted slowly across the river, I took the opportunity to discourse with the ferry pilot about his profession. Despite his innate cupidity, he proved quite affable once we had arrived mid-stream, and our safe conveyance appeared a given. I asked him about the potential perils of his profession. He said, "If everything is right, well, there's not much to it. But if you have one of them windy, rainy, dark nights, you can't see, and the water's up—well, just everybody can't do it."

When we finally arrived in San Antonio that Thursday, the first of June 1865, the first thing we saw was the Alamo itself. The stage disembarked right across from Alamo Plaza, and I could see that famous old Spanish mission where so much bloodshed had occurred just a year shy of thirty years earlier. It appeared much smaller than I had imagined. Still, I resolved to visit on the first occasion to pay homage to the patriots who had fought and died there, including the likes of William Travis, Davy Crockett, and, of course, my own local hero, James Bowie of Logan County, Kentucky.

A gentleman on the stage from New Orleans had told me about a reputable boarding house near Alamo Plaza run by a kind widower called Mrs. Adams. He said to mention his name, and she would welcome me there as well as Mary, now traveling as a formerly enslaved person and my paid personal lady's maid. But he warned us that enslaved people in Texas had not yet been freed, and many southern slaveholders were migrating to Texas for that very reason (being the farthest western bastion of the Confederate states). The war may have officially ended when General Lee surrendered in Virginia, not to mention the Emancipation Proclamation from '63, but such news traveled slowly to Texas. Once again, Mary was obliged to assume the ruse of enslaved servant to a traveling Southern lady.

Upon arriving at Adams' Boarding House, my request for room and board found purchase, and we were soon settled in comfortable lodgings with a balcony view of the Plaza. The cost of room and board (including two meals each per day) was seventy-five cents a person. Mrs. Adams said supper was served promptly at 6:00 p.m. and breakfast at 7:00 a.m. She looked at Mary apologetically.

"Your servant will naturally take her meals in the room."

I was shocked to hear this. "But I thought..."

"I know the war's ended," Mrs. Adams interrupted, "with General Lee's surrender up at Appomattox, but many folks refuse to accept the truth of their defeat. It's all I can do to permit colored folk, freed or otherwise, into my house."

I was angry now. "Then I'll stay in the room with Mary!" I insisted. But it was Mary who talked me out of it.

She said, "Don't you worry about me none, Miss Carlotta. You go on to supper now. You never know who you might meet!"

"Please do, Miss Tompkins," Mrs. Adams insisted. "The house is unusually full this evening, and the company should be very lively!"

I looked again at Mary, who nodded encouragingly.

At 6:00 sharp, the dinner bell rang out, and Mrs. Adams' shrill voice called from the bottom of the stairwell: "Supper's ready! Y'all come on, now!" She was not mistaken about the lively company, which proved larger than could be accommodated at the dining room table. Mrs. Adams scurried to join another table to it as a makeshift extension, covering it with a plain bedsheet in stark contrast to the fine linen tablecloth on the main table. She then scrambled to locate additional chairs of various sizes from an adjacent room to ensure everyone had a place to sit. At last, each person had a spot, and as I reached for my chair, I was startled when it seemed to move of its own accord.

"Allow me," said a man behind me on my right. I turned to see a fashionably dressed gentleman with a prominent black mustache smiling at me as he gestured for me to sit. I did so, and after straightening my dress, I turned back to thank him, but he had vanished, only to reappear on my left at the head of the table. I felt suddenly moved by his gesture, which reminded me of home—and of the seemingly lost art of gentlemanly manners I had often missed amongst the rather uncouth men who lurked in gambling halls.

The room was lit by a large kerosene lamp amid the table, which cast a reddish-gold glimmer upon the faces present. I glanced back at the gentleman who had seated me and was struck by how his eyes seemed to glint in the lamplight in contrast to his jet-dark hair that matched his mustache. I secretly hoped that he might speak to me again. (I would hear him speak again that evening, all right, but not to me.)

Once grace was said and the food was being passed around the table, Mrs. Adams made the obligatory apology about the food that I had heard countless times from Mama (which I knew was just her way of "fishing for compliments").

She said, "Now I'm sorry about the biscuits. I did my best with them, but they just aren't fit to eat."

This, of course, netted the desired response, with most everyone at the table praising her biscuits as the best they had ever put in their mouths.

Shortly into the meal, and before the company had been properly introduced to one another, a skirmish arose between North and South over a matter of indisputable importance. The subject of contention? A pan of cornbread. It started innocently enough when a young Union veteran seated at the far end of the table politely asked the man adjacent if he would pass the bread. But after a black skillet of cornbread was handed to him, things went south. The young man glared at the man next to him.

He asked, "What is this?"

"That is the bread."

"That is not bread. I refuse to eat this southern slop. Pass me some real bread!"

At that, the table fell dead silent. Mrs. Adams looked crestfallen. The following person to speak was the gentleman at the head of the table to my left, with sparkling eyes and a dark mustache. He said:

"That is called cornbread, boy, and it is the finest bread you'll ever taste. You will eat every last crumb of it too, you damn Yankee, before you may be excused from the table."

"I declare that I will not," said the young man defiantly, pushing the pan away with a sneer of disgust. But when he looked back up, he was staring at the barrel of a gun.

"I declare that you will." The gentleman to my left was now pointing his pistol directly at the soldier's face. Something about his demeanor must have seemed convincing to the young man because—with shaking hand—he now reached back to the skillet and slowly pulled it to him. He took out the remaining large piece of cornbread and devoured it as everyone watched in nervous anticipation. When he had finished it, the gentleman with the gun stood up.

"Now get the hell out, and never come back to this house."

The young soldier complied, quickly pushing back his chair and stepping cautiously to the door before hastening away. It was not until we heard the front door open and close and the sound of his footsteps stomping down the wooden steps that the gentleman put away his gun, resumed his seat, and smiled at Mrs. Adams.

"It appears we shall need some more cornbread," he said, and with that, our dinner resumed as if nothing untoward had just occurred. I noted, however, that every last person finished the cornbread on their plate (like it or not) as if their life depended on it!

The next morning at breakfast, as Mrs. Adams poured my coffee, I asked her about the previous evening.

"Who was that gentleman at supper last night? The one who so valiantly defended your cornbread?"

She answered, "I don't rightly know, but around

here, they call him 'Cherokee' Frank. He's taken a liking to my cooking and comes here to supper now and then. Says it reminds him of his mama's vittles back home."

I was now all the more intrigued by this dark, handsome, and mysterious stranger. Yet, it would not be too long before our paths crossed once again.

In the meantime, major social change was afoot around us, which was of special import to Mary. General Robert E. Lee's surrender and the war's consequent end had finally caught up to Texas. Within a few weeks of our arrival, the news arrived from Galveston that Federal troops had arrived in Texas and Union Army General Gordon Granger, the new Federal commander of the Department of Texas, had issued his "General Order Number 3":

"The people of Texas are informed that, in accordance with a proclamation from the Executive of the United States, all slaves are free. This involves an absolute equality of personal rights and rights of property between former masters and slaves, and the connection heretofore existing between them becomes that between employer and hired labor."

This was the news for which Mary and I had been waiting! Now, we could finally cast aside the old ruse once and for all. The city was filled with jubilation, as formerly-enslaved men, women and children danced and sang in the streets. The unbridled joy in people's faces was a sight to behold. That was on Monday, the nineteenth of June, a day that would soon become celebrated annually as "Juneteenth" in commemoration of the emancipation of slaves in Texas.

The joy was, alas, short-lived. Texas was filled to the brim with now ex-Confederate enslavers, who were not about to accept Lee's surrender and the end of the war lightly. Many defied the authorities (and, increasingly, the reality of history) by whipping their slaves into continued submission—while shooting and lynching those who attempted to flee. They regarded with contempt anyone who dared to comply by setting their own slaves free, or especially—as stipulated in Order Number 3—making the "connection heretofore existing between them that between employer and hired labor." So Mary and I had to continue walking a tightrope publicly, lest we incur the wrath of those who would harm us for simply following the law.

Nevertheless, I now relied upon Mary all the more in her old role as guardian, especially being a young woman alone in an unknown city at a time of social turmoil. I had found employment (courtesy of a referral by Mrs. Adams) conducting poker games at the nearby Cosmopolitan Club casino and saloon. Mrs. Adams had warned me, however, that it could draw a drunken crowd of rowdy roughnecks and cowhands and other assorted riffraff (such folk as Mama would call "trash"). Many of them were exiled Confederate soldiers now seething with rage over the recent turn of events.

Mary sat behind me on a stool as my "lookout" as I dealt the cards each night at the Cosmopolitan. From there, she would lour over the table at the gamblers seated around me, who, more often than not, appeared visibly disgruntled about it and frequently complained. But Mary held her ground, and I felt all the safer for it, confident that her mere presence was enough to make any man think twice about misbehaving.

Until one evening, that is, when a white-bearded fellow dressed in the remnants of a tattered gray Confederate uniform decided to try his luck. He had just lost the round when he angrily slapped his cards upon the table and stared hard at Mary from beneath the rim of his bullet-ridden and partially burned hat. I saw he had a crude tattoo of the rebel flag atop his hand, with which he was now pointing at her as he spoke with a rustic Southern twang.

"How much for yer slave?"

I attempted to ignore him, although the other men around the table perked up in hopes of a scene. Sure enough, the old rebel was just getting started.

"I asked you a question, little vixen. I said, how much for that giant slave of yours there atop the stool?"

Without raising my eyes from the cards I was now busy dealing, I replied: "Have you not heard the news, mister? The war's over, and slavery is ended."

He took out a silver money clip stuffed with notes and placed it in the pot. "This right here says it ain't. If I win this hand, she's mine."

He leered at Mary, who shot him back the meanest evil eye I had ever yet seen from her. But she resisted adding fuel to the fire by responding and wisely kept her mouth shut. Then he added, "All nine fingers of her." This provoked a chuckle among the assorted group at the table, none of whom appeared inclined to come to my aid if necessary. I began to feel a knot of anxiety welling up in my stomach, as I could see the man fidgeting with something under the table I imagined must be a weapon of some sort. I nevertheless attempted to remain calm.

"As I said, sir, the war is now over, and my friend is not for sale."

The man gave a cold laugh. "Your friend, is she? I reckon that figures, don't it, for a little bitch like you! I have a mind to give you the whuppin' you deserve for keeping such 'friends' as that."

This was too much for Mary. She leaned over toward the man and gave him a look so hard that he averted his eyes despite himself and his tough-man façade.

"You take that back, Mistah, right now! You don't know who you be talkin' to here. Miss Carlotta is a lady the likes such trash as you ain't never seen."

At that, the man jumped up, and so did Mary, who towered over him menacingly. The only difference was that he now held a gun and appeared ready to use it without a moment's thought. But right then, another voice joined in, and I recognized it immediately: It was that of "Cherokee" Frank standing at the table, who now gestured to the man to lower his gun.

He said, "There appears to be some misunderstanding here." He looked at the gun. "Especially from you, mister. Maybe you misread the sign at the entrance, the one that says such toys ain't allowed inside the club. They must be checked upon entering. You may now be excused from the table." He gave the man the same ineluctable glare as he had the Yankee with the cornbread, and it was once again sufficient. The angry old Reb grumbled under his breath and put away the gun, but he proceeded to grab his money back from the pot before making a quick exit. I looked back at Frank, perhaps a bit too admiringly.

"I did not realize you worked here."

"I don't," he replied, smiling. "It just seemed you might need some assistance."

"For that, I am very much obliged!"

"This is my club." He took a card from his inside coat pocket and placed it gently in my hand. It read: "University Club. Frank Thurmond, Proprietor."

7

I HAD BY NOW SUFFICIENTLY PROFITED from my winnings at the Cosmopolitan Club to secure my own lodgings: a small rent house on San Pedro Street in the business district. It was a quaint old building constructed of adobe in the Spanish colonial style, with a red tile roof.

On the nights I was free from my Cosmopolitan Club table, I soon took to frequenting the San Antonio theatre on Market Street known as Casino Hall. There, I attended some of the finest drama, concerts, ballet, and opera then being performed by American (and sometimes even international) performing troupes on tour at that time. I did this for some much-needed cultural edification as well as the need to establish at least a semblance of social credibility otherwise ill-served by my current occupation. Casino Hall was a grand new theatre then, with an impressive interior designed in imitation of the Russian Bolshoi Theatre, complete with numerous private boxes draped with red velvet curtains and overlooking the stage from high above. It was lit by majestic crystal chandeliers that sparkled like stars in the candlelight. An enchanting place it was, especially when the atmosphere was charged with exquisite music, drama, and dance.

There was, of course, no escaping completely the opinion of my detractors, mostly “aristocratic” women who had simply managed to marry well, often to much older men to whom they had once been of particular “service.” (I had to admit, however, my own occasional yearning for the right fellow to come along and save me from my rather desperate plight as a lady gambler in a strange land.) Yet, for the most part, I succeeded in “making a splash” courtesy of the Southern belle demeanor of my roots, combined with my fashionable New Orleans clothes. I found myself invited to many an evening soirée too, held among the highest echelons of San Antonio’s social elite.

Despite my hopes, however, I never once came across the mysterious “Cherokee” Frank again on any of these occasions. If he were ever present at the theatre or elsewhere, I did not see him. Finally, after another year quickly passed along with many an evening pondering his card in the quiet hours of the night, I resolved to pay a visit to his club.

It was not at all usual then for a lady to turn up alone at a private gambling club such as the University

Club (or even the most run-of-the-mill saloon, for that matter). But I was at least in possession of the proprietor's card, which I figured must surely count for something.

It turned out that the University Club was on a side street just off Alamo Plaza, and so it was with a thrilling sense of adventurous trepidation that I strolled right up to the front door early one evening and walked in. Two shotgun-toting guards keeping watch on either side of the entrance regarded me warily but did nothing to hinder my passage.

The first thing I noticed was the money stacked in piles on most every table. I had never seen such a copious amount of money in one place! No wonder the entrance was guarded. There was indeed so much money in the form of gold and silver coinage that bucketloads of coins were dumped into wheelbarrows for transfer between tables, where—as I later learned—well-to-do ranchers and bankers and such that owned property around town laid bets on stakes higher than I had ever yet come across.

I was soon confronted by a rather eccentric-looking old porter in a tuxedo topped with a black bowler hat. If a walrus ever took a notion to mate with a penguin, such a creature as he would be the result. He was as Victorian a gentleman in both demeanor and appearance as I had ever yet encountered, sporting an English-style mustache whose twisted ends culminated in a pair of stupendous sideburns. His appearance was matched with an elegantly formal British accent, in stark contrast to the local Texas drawl. The look he gave me was one of amused insouciance.

"May I be of assistance, madam?" he asked, then curtly added: "Looking for someone in particular, are you?"

Summoning up my courage, I carefully extracted the card from my purse and showed it to him. "Yes, I am. As a matter of fact, I was hoping you might direct me to this gentleman."

The name on the card clearly took him by surprise. "So it's Mr. Frank you are after, is it?" I just nodded as he regarded me somewhat suspiciously for a moment. Then he discreetly gestured across the room, where I could just make out the bar wreathed in a thick cloud of smoke. "The tall fellow at the bar standing nearest the piano, he of the rather odd-looking hat—that will be your man."

As I made my way through the room among the many tables, I did my best to appear confident (albeit feeling far from it beneath the forced smile)—all the while attempting to seem oblivious to the many eyes I felt watching me as I passed through the crowded floor. Somewhere, almost lost within the loud din of men's voices, was the tinkle of notes emanating from the piano by the bar, which became louder as I approached (though whatever music it was escapes me now). When I reached the long, polished mahogany bar with burnished brass rails, "Mr. Frank" was coaxing a lit match into igniting the tobacco of an ornately carved burl wood pipe.

Preoccupied with his puffing, it was with an expression of befuddled surprise that he responded to my approach. He hastily shook out the match, tapped out his pipe in a tray, and stood up to his full height. He wore a hat unlike any I had yet seen: It was wide-brimmed and high crowned—encircled with a shiny silver band around the bottom—and made of pearl-gray felt that made me long to reach up and touch it (though I well knew a man's hat was ever strictly off limits). He now doffed it courteously to me, as I tried my darndest to appear demure despite a sudden sensation of excitement—especially when he took my hand, and I felt his lips gently touch it with a kiss. At that moment, my skin tingled well-nigh all over, and I hoped the goosebumps on my arms were not too visible.

"Miss Carlotta, if my memory holds true?"

"Your memory is sound, sir. Though I do not recall ever being properly introduced."

He smiled. "I confess I took the liberty of inquiring about you at Mrs. Adams' boarding house—after that little adventure at the Cosmopolitan, which now seems so long ago! I had hoped maybe to encounter you again over dinner there, only to discover you had moved elsewhere."

Something about his revelation rendered me rather breathless at that moment. I felt my heartbeat accelerate and found it difficult to speak. "That is true. I now live with my friend and personal servant, Mary, on San Pedro Street."

He regarded my face closely with a look of some concern. "You appear flushed," he remarked, then called to the bartender: a younger man standing apart behind the bar polishing a tankard while thinly attempting to disguise his eavesdropping upon our conversation. "Hey, Will! A fan for the lady, please."

"Sure thing, Frank!" The young man opened a drawer beneath the bar and produced a long, folded fan, which he handed to Frank, who opened it to reveal beautifully decorative art depicting a snow-capped mountain surrounded by what I took to be Japanese characters. I looked at it admiringly before remembering its primary function of soughing up a breeze. Frank seemed pleased to see me so immediately taken with it.

"A visiting Japanese gentleman gave that to us. Said them letters relate some sort of poem, something he called a "'high koo'"–by a poet named ... I forget the name."

"Basho, maybe?" I conjectured. "I read some haiku in school!"

"Yep! That was it. Basho." He exchanged a nod with Will. "The gentleman wrote down a translation for us at the time, though I seem to have misplaced it. Fortunately, I had already taken the poem to heart."

He gathered himself as if delivering a formal speech, and then began to recite:

"Canopy of snow–
Even the birds are silent.
White cat vanishes."

"That's lovely!"

"The fan is yours to keep. Our little gift to you."

"Much obliged to you both!" By this time, I had stirred up a soft breeze with the fan and felt a measure calmer.

Frank gestured toward Will, a towheaded young

man who was now busy measuring out shots of whiskey for customers at the bar. "That is my little brother, William Russell. He and my older brother, Harrison, run the place with me." He stooped slightly to replace his hat, caught me staring at it, and grinned.

"You like my hat?"

"I was just admiring it, I do not recall ever seeing such a hat."

"That is because you haven't. This just arrived as a promotion from an enterprising new hatter up in Philadelphia, a man named Stetson. He calls this new style 'the Boss of the Plains.' My brothers joke about it, naturally. But I reckon I'll have the last laugh when these hats start selling like hotcakes, and I own one straight from Mr. Stetson's very first batch!"

"Well, I think it suits you just fine."

He gave me a quick half-tip of his hat and smiled again. Then he said, "Why don't we step into the reception room? It will be quieter in there, and I have a little proposition that may well be of interest to you."

The reception room was about as posh a place I had ever seen (especially in San Antonio), though a tad bit gaudy in terms of décor. It reminded me of the living room in my family mansion back home, including the beautiful baby grand piano. The room was secluded from the hustle and bustle of the saloon and casino as a separate parlor of its own, which opened in turn into several additional rooms, their separate entrances draped with decoratively fringed red curtains drawn up like ribbons in a young girl's hair. One of them was occupied by a large snooker table, around which two young men with cue sticks paced eagerly, taking their respective turns at potting various colored balls. I could just make out a stack of bills adorning the table's edge.

Frank showed me to a French-style armchair with comfortably soft velvet upholstery, then for himself took one adjacent. There was a small table of dark wood with ornate legs between us, on which he placed a tall bottle and two glasses he had brought from the bar. I recognized the label at once. It was a bottle of 1859 Kentucky bourbon whiskey.

I said, "A nice little memento of home."

He grinned. "I heard you were from Kentucky. Thought you might like a taste of it again." Frank uncorked the bottle and offered to pour me a drink.

"I don't mind if I do!"

He proceeded to pour a nifty portion into the glass. "Proper Kentucky bourbon has been mighty hard to come by since the war. Fortunately, we saw fit to stock up when we could." He then poured an even fuller glass for himself. "Best be careful, sugar, this stuff is known to pack a wallop."

"I can handle my libations, mister," I said.

He raised his glass. "To Kentucky."

"To Kentucky!"

Frank reached inside his jacket pocket and took out his pipe along with a small paper sack, from which he extracted a generous pinch of tobacco and filled the bowl of his pipe. Then he placed the stem between his lips and struck a match upon the sole of his boot. He carefully lit the tobacco with a series of quick puffs until the bowl glowed with a soft red warmth. The resulting smoke, with its rich and pungent scent tinged with an apple sweetness, pleased me. It reminded me of Daddy on quiet Sunday afternoons after church and dinner.

As he thoughtfully smoked his pipe, Frank managed to ask between puffs: "Being from Kentucky, I don't suppose the name of Bowie has escaped your attention?"

"Jim Bowie is among my true heroes!" I said excitedly. "Everyone back home simply reveres him."

"Then I presume you might recognize this here little trinket." He reached his left arm behind his neck and pulled out a large blade of some nine inches in length. It had a short wooden handle attached to a lanyard. He laid it carefully on the table in front of me, and the blade glinted in the lamplight.

I had always heard about such knives but had never seen one. "A Bowie knife!" I exclaimed. I was as much impressed by his knowledge of Bowie's Kentucky origins as by the knife itself.

"The same," said Frank. "I got it from an old bladesmith called James Black up in Arkansas. Same fella who forged the original blade for your hero Bowie that he wielded at yonder Alamo." He gestured in no particular direction.

Observing my curiosity as I glanced at the string upon which the knife was affixed to his person, he said: "We have a strict rule forbidding weapons of any kind inside the Club." He chuckled and added: "Such rules, however, tend to fly over the hat of your average Texan. I rest easier knowing this here blade has my back." He carefully lifted the knife over his head and slid it gingerly back into a leather sheath concealed beneath his jacket.

"But what on earth brings a lady like you to a gambling hell such as this?"

"It's what I do. I learnt to play from my daddy, and after he died in the war, plying the pasteboards was the only way I could provide for my mother and sister."

"Are they still in Kentucky?"

"Mama's dead now, too. My sister Ellie Mae is in finishing school, for which I send her money from here."

"Very noble of you, to be sure. I have a couple of sisters myself."

"What are their names?"

Frank smiled. "The youngest is called Barbara Ann. Sweet as a peach she is, and Lord, do I miss her. She's still back home helping our papa on the farm. Barbara's very well-read, too, just as I take it you are. And then there's Jenny Kate." Now he frowned. "She seems cut from an altogether different cloth than the rest of us. Quite a mess, Jenny is!"

"Where is Jenny Kate now?"

Frank shook his head disapprovingly. "Here with us in San Antonio, alas. Daddy could no longer abide her saucy tongue and sent her packing to Texas with me and the boys. She has, I fear, become known as somewhat of a troublemaker about town. Her heart's in the right place, certainly. But her methods, well ..." He shook his head sadly a moment before quickly changing the subject. "Yet enough about me, pray tell more of yourself–and of Kentucky."

I took another sip of whiskey and felt the sensation

of warmth fill my chest as the liquid coursed down my throat, while its effect heightened my perception of the moment and subdued my wonted inhibition. I found myself telling this intriguing stranger all about the family plantation, my childhood there, my schooling, and Daddy's horses. I included what happened after war broke out, Daddy's death, and my move with Mary to Detroit and eventually down river to New Orleans.

Yet, for some reason, I never found the inclination to tell Frank about Johnny Golden, and how it was he who had asked me to come ultimately to San Antonio. Much less that he planned to meet me there, something I had nearly forgotten myself and had long ago begun both to doubt and even to dread. But still, there had been no word or sign from Johnny since Detroit, so that I now felt sure he must have perished in the war.

It was getting late by this time, and despite my best efforts to suppress it, a yawn forced its way upon me. Frank drew out a pocket watch upon a fine silver fob chain that hung in a loop from his waistcoat pocket to his belt.

He said, "The hour is getting late, and I must insist upon walking you home. First, however, there is still my little proposition. How would you like to come work for us?"

This took me by surprise, and for once, I was at a loss for words. He continued:

"I have seen you play cards. Your daddy taught you well. Lady gamblers, and seemingly virtuous ones at that, are not at all easy to find. Especially in Texas." He winked.

"What of my work at the Cosmopolitan?"

"What of it? Leave it! You are much above that place. Here you will find a better clientele, and one with more money to lose as well! From whose losses, I must add, you will receive a generous percentage from the winnings."

He went on to describe some spectacular house winnings over the years, but I was hardly even listening by that point. I had already made up my mind. (Not only, I began now to perceive, solely for the job itself.)

I nodded wearily. "I accept." He held out his hand, and I shook it with an exaggerated formality.

"You'll be respected around town as the 'queen of the pasteboards' in no time," he said, and stood up to escort me home. But as we proceeded through the reception room, I could not help but pause by the piano, so much did I miss playing.

He asked, "Do you play?"

"Once upon a time. But I must be very rusty now."

"Nonsense! Won't you play something for me before we leave? We had it tuned only this week."

I hesitated uncertainly for a second or two, then nodded resolutely to myself and sat upon the bench, flexed my hands as if clearing cobwebs from between my fingers, and listened a moment in silence to summon up the remembrance of songs past. Something about that moment sitting in front of a keyboard again, after so many years away from my beloved piano of childhood, lent itself to a certain lugubriousness, as a distinct melody welled up from somewhere deep within. What I heard in my mind's ear was the "Prelude in E minor" by

Chopin, and at that moment, my fingers responded to my thoughts and began to express what I heard inside. As I played, the music took me back in memory through all the places I had seen since leaving home: from the northern industrial city of Detroit; the trip downriver the length of the Mississippi with all the many contrasts of people and landscapes, and the cruel ravages of war glimpsed upon both sides of the river; the charming gaiety of New Orleans despite it all; to now the wild world of Texas on the frontier's edge. I had already seen and experienced more than most any young woman could ever have done then. Yet something told me my true journey had only just begun.

When I reached the end of the Prelude with its lingering minor chord, I glanced over my shoulder just in time to see Frank wipe a tear from his eye. I looked quickly back down at the keyboard and smiled thoughtfully to myself. Despite carrying himself as the kind of man one wouldn't wish to cry in front of, he was clearly, at heart, a sensitive soul!

Outside, the street was illuminated by occasional streetlamps, around whose kerosene flames hovered a fine autumn mist like scarlet halos. It was a good mile home, and the pace of our walk was by no means rushed as we passed by darkened storefronts along both sides of the dusty road. The air was filled with the raucous melody of countless tree frogs chirping. Along the way, I asked Frank if he would not tell me something of his own past. "And why, may I ask, do they call you 'Cherokee' Frank?" Upon my last question, he glanced at me a moment with a smile that betrayed a hint of wistfulness before commencing his tale.

He was born in Georgia on November 21, 1840. His father, Jason C. Thurmond (known affectionately as "J.C."), had grown up there himself, his family being originally from Wilkes County, North Carolina. Frank was especially proud that his grandfather Thomas Thurmond had fought in the Revolutionary War, along with all of his brothers. Frank's father had met and married his mother, Mary Stokes, while farming in Jackson County, near the old Georgia Indian Lands.

"Ma's kin were all Cherokee, hence that particular nickname you mentioned! Most of them was rounded up and herded off to reservations in the Oklahoma territory on Andrew Jackson's murderous Trail of Tears. That was in about 1836, when Pa married my mother to save her ..." Frank momentarily choked up, then continued: "From the deliberate slaughter of her people. I was only about eight years old when Pa moved us to Mississippi in '49 so Ma could be with some of her family that managed to escape and remain behind there. That was in Choctaw County. And that is where I grew up, where we labored on the land as sharecroppers."

I looked at him anxiously. "Did your family own slaves?"

He chuckled to himself. "Hell no, we was way too poor for that! Money for us was scarce as angels' wings. Might as well been slaves ourselves, the way them landowners there treated us. So when the war come along, my brothers and me—well, we just saw it as our one big chance to escape the farm. I had just turned twenty-one when we all volunteered with the Confederate army. Harrison was twenty-two then, but William Russell was not yet eighteen, though said he was and got through with no further questions. We each wound up in different regiments, and I heard neither hide nor hare of my brothers for some time after. I could only hope their luck held out wherever they were.

"My own luck almost run out in Tennessee at the Battle of Stones River, near Murfreesboro. There, in the midst of battle, I was hunkered down with my regiment in a shallow trench we'd dug near the front line. A rumble of cannon blasts in front of us was so close I could feel the ground tremble. Then I heard it: a whistling sound like someone calling his horse, before the mortar shell exploded not much farther off than that storefront yonder just ahead of us. If something hadn't told me to drop flat to the dirt at that very moment, I would not be here to tell the tale. Suddenly the pain struck. I thought for a moment I'd just been snakebit after feeling a sharp pinch in my left leg. Then such a horrible piercing pain shot up my leg I thought I must have lost it in the blast. But once the smoke cleared, I could see a shard of shrapnel sticking out from my skin just above the knee. I noticed blood spattered all around me, and when I turned to check on the soldier next to me, a young fella from Alabama called Jessie, there was just a stump where his head once was. It reminded me of watching as a child on the farm when Pa beheaded chickens with his ax on a tree stump—the way they looked, running headless away, their legs a-pumping. I thought it funny then, never thinking such could happen to a fellow man.

"After the battle, they took me to one of them makeshift hospital tents. It was covered in dirt after the battle, and inside were men with their innards exposed, pleading in agony for their mothers. The morphine was all out, and not even a bottle of whiskey could be found to help ease the terrible suffering. They laid me on a dirty blanket and stuffed a rag in my mouth to stifle my screams as they cut out the shrapnel from my leg. I knew what was coming when I saw the surgeon on duty produce a bone saw and walk my way. Well, I wasn't about to let them take my leg and made it known by unsheathing my sword and pointing it at the surgeon's throat. I said, 'You touch so much as a hair on my leg, and that will be the last thing you ever do!'

"He tried to reason with me, saying that I would surely lose both my leg and my life once the gangrene set in. I said I would take my chances, and so he let me be. I went back home to Mississippi after that, and, sure enough, recovered sufficiently to fight again that summer at Gettysburg. I have something of a limp to this day, but at least I am still walking on two legs!"

I had observed that Frank walked with a slight limp, but it was hardly noticeable and now seemed rather remarkable upon knowing the story behind it.

He continued: "By the end of the war, I was a Union prisoner. But they sent me home last spring after General Lee's surrender and the war's end. Both of my brothers managed to survive and were already there. That is when—after seeing enough of the ravages of war in Sherman's wake and the hardship and misery of

'Reconstruction' afterward–we saw fit to head west to Texas."

At this, I concurred. "I understand too well about war. Nothing was the same again for me or my family after Daddy was killed."

Frank gave an empathetic nod. "We promised to send help home to Ma and Pa in Mississippi just as soon as we could, and we have made good on that promise. Harrison is on his way home even now with as much money and goods as he can carry. However, it weren't easy at first. We cowboyed a spell as ranchers in south Texas, and then gambled our way around the frontier at the likes of Fort Chadbourne and Fort Worth. Finally we come to San Antonio and won the University Club in a high stakes game. One which, if we had lost, would have seen us still on the run as we speak! I had just recently arrived in San Antonio when you first saw me at Mrs. Adam's boarding house. Now our casino is known as amongst the best this side of the Mississippi."

He glanced at me with a twinkle in his eye. "Soon, I might add, to boast a lovely new attraction as well."

Frank had just finished his story when we arrived outside the house on San Pedro Street. The windows were dark, so I figured Mary had turned in to bed early. What happened next has remained foggy in my memory ever since (due partly no doubt to that evening's bourbon acting upon my will), but the last thing I remembered clearly upon awakening the following morning was that of falling into Frank's arms. And that I felt safe there, too. I could not, however, recall if the occasion of a kiss had transpired between us. (I immediately feared it was so, but then another part of me interjected with the hope that it had happened indeed and was not just my imagination getting away from me.) Or maybe it was all, in fact, just a dream.

One thing was sure, though: My next encounter with Frank was bound to feel awkward, whether there had or had not happened the occurrence of a kiss. It was the unknowing that felt so unbearable.

8

THE SOUND OF A KEY TURNING in the door startled me. It was Mary, just now getting home following a full night out. She must have noticed a quizzical expression in my eyes because she immediately became defensive.

"Now don't you be judging, Miss Carlotta, ain't nothin' to worry about with me."

I decided not to reply and only nodded, as she was completely free now to come and go at will with no questions asked, from me or anyone else. However, seeing my concern prompted further explanation upon her own accord. It seemed she had gotten involved with an association of formerly enslaved women and various other local women who made it their purpose to help the orphans of the city (children of the enslaved and otherwise) learn to survive by stealing food and other goods. I was especially surprised to learn that one of the ringleaders of the group was Jenny Kate Thurmond. Frank's sister! I recalled his description of her as a "troublemaker about town"—but from Mary's point of view, they were involved in a noble cause that she, along with Jenny Kate and the others, passionately believed in. I was inclined to agree and saw fit only to caution her to take good care (especially knowing how many of the locals would readily seize upon any excuse to prosecute and arrest—and worse—the enslaved who were recently freed).

That afternoon, I sashayed into the University Club with all the confidence I could muster. I had gone shopping and bought myself a new hat at the only millinery shop in town that stocked the latest fashions as soon as they arrived from New Orleans. The first thing I noticed when I arrived at the Club was the new deference with which I was, this time, met by the "gatekeepers" of the place. The two guards standing watch outside the entrance both tipped their hats as I walked in. Once inside, even the old penguin of a porter acknowledged me with a curt nod—though his bowler hat remained firmly rooted atop his round head.

When I reached the bar, a friendly smile greeted me. I said, "Hello! William Russell, is it not?"

"Miss Carlotta," he answered politely, putting down the silver tankard he was polishing. "And just call me Will."

He grinned again, and I was struck by the authenticity of his expressive smile. Will Thurmond seemed a young man to be trusted. In many ways, he favored his older brother Frank, but there was a real charm about him, too, enhanced by the long, wavy locks that fell in golden curls about his neck. He had lovely gray eyes, in contrast with the hazel eyes of his brother.

"Frank is expecting you, he's in the lounge." Will gestured toward the reception room where I had met with Frank the previous day. I thanked him and turned to go, but then heard Will's voice again behind me as I stepped away from the bar.

"He's quite smitten with you, you know." I pretended not to hear, though inwardly felt a secret thrill.

The first thing Frank did was to show me a "Faro" box sitting on the table. He asked, "Do you know how to deal Faro?"

"I have observed many a Faro table in action, but never yet sat behind one."

Frank laid the cards in their places on the card layout. "An old French card game, brought to America by English aristocrats and now all the rage in the West." He picked up a random card and pointed to the tiger illustration on it. "They call it 'Bucking the Tiger' after that Bengal tiger on the back of every card."

"I will do my best to learn it!" I exclaimed excitedly.

"I'll teach you the art of dealing Faro with finesse. In the meantime, how are you at Five Card Stud?"

"That is my specialty."

"Excellent. You will start tonight!"

I now eyed Frank intently. I said, "I have but one condition."

Frank looked at me, surprised. "And what is that?"

"I require that Mary still be allowed to sit behind me as my lookout."

Frank appeared taken aback at this and scratched his head in thought. He finally answered, albeit reluctantly: "I fear our clientele will not be inclined to approve."

"It is non-negotiable."

"So be it," he sighed. "I was mighty impressed with the way she stood up to that ruffian fellow at the Cosmopolitan!"

I was very pleased with this turn of events, as Faro was considered far classier than run-of-the mill draw poker, and I had long desired the opportunity of a Faro table to myself. Frank had promised to teach me how to deal Faro, and in the meantime set me to flipping the pasteboards at my poker table. I was given ample money by the house to deal with each evening, and—just as Frank had promised—received a generous percentage of the winnings as a house gambler.

Mary took her place once more sitting on a stool just behind me as lookout, ready to flash her infamous "evil eye" at any patron gambler she suspected of trying to cheat, or who otherwise may have seemed any potential threat to me. There were the usual hurtful epithets, but Mary had long ago steeled her nerves against such insults. For her, it was the potential violence that lurked beneath those words that remained the chief concern.

One day, I got so fed up that I made a rule against cussing—or the use otherwise of any inappropriate language, especially against Mary—at my table. (The taking of the Lord's name in vain is something else that I would not abide.) With Mary's help I was able to enforce this policy too, and after that the word got around real quick that any man gambling at my table at least need be polite or would be deprived of his seat. The constant drinking and smoking were certainly bad enough, but there is only so much one can ask in a saloon—however "classy" it liked to call itself.

It did not take long in the meantime for news to get around of the mysterious new beauty with flaming red locks and dark eyes dealing Faro at the University Club. After only a few weeks, my table there was drawing gamblers from many miles around, just like moths fluttering about a flame in the darkest night.

It was Will who informed me at the bar one day of the new nickname I had acquired. He said, "Have you heard what they are calling you about town, Miss Carlotta?"

"I cannot say that I have."

"They call you 'the Angel of San Antonio'."

I smiled. It was a catchy little sobriquet and somewhat flattering to boot.

Once I settled into my work at the University Club, time seemed to pass by quickly. It was already the autumn of '67, and my coffers were filled to the brim with winnings, enough so that I was able to buy my own small but cozy house. The cottage was large enough for Mary and me to each have our own bedroom for once. It was the first time I finally had a real space to myself since leaving home, while, of course, Mary was particularly pleased.

Speaking of home, after sending money to Kentucky for Ellie Mae's final year of school, I received a letter back from my sister with the surprise news that she was married in secret to a young gentleman of good family there who had managed to keep his inheritance money safely hidden during the war. (It had been buried deep beneath the servants' outhouse where, as hoped, nobody had been much inclined to look.) While his family home was completely burned to the ground during the Union occupation, our own mansion had remained standing—thanks mostly to having served as the local headquarters of federal troops. They planned to live there and to rebuild the old farm. Her new husband was also fond of horses and determined to resume racing at Daddy's old track just as soon as possible. I was, of course, delighted with the news and wrote back to my sister to tell her so. It was just what our parents had always wanted for me too, of course.

But I felt gratified to know that, with my help, Ellie Mae had survived the war with her schooling completed and that we had fulfilled our parents' ultimate wishes by keeping the family estate and business intact. I told my sister in turn that things were going well with my "Texas cattleman." Little had I ever imagined when I first told her that concocted story how near the mark it would one day hit! I missed my little sister terribly, but though I did not then wish to admit it to myself, I still somehow knew that I would never see her (or home) ever again.

Ellie Mae's marriage meant that I no longer had to worry about sending money back home and could now keep all of my winnings. Mary, who was eager to find paid employment of her own, was now free to do so.

One night, about a month after the commencement of my work at the Club, Frank took me to a local restaurant near the Plaza. The night was unseasonably warm, and tables were set outside with a good view of the Alamo. The old stone walls of that grand Spanish mission glowed orange in the flickering torchlight, while the dark sky above was illumined by stars like countless ethereal diamonds. The restaurant was a Mexican tavern, complete with a mariachi band serenading the patrons from beneath enormous, colorful sombreros.

As steaming dishes were brought to our table, Frank gestured at the food. He said, "It's high time you were introduced to the delights of Mexican cuisine."

"I have never dared to try it before now!"

Frank served me from one of the dishes. "Best to be careful, the real stuff is too hot for your average gringo. It will knock your hat off!"

"The real stuff?"

"This here's milder than the authentic habanero-laden fare. I call it Texian-Mexican."

"In other words, you reckon I cannot handle the real hot stuff?"

"That is not what I meant ..." stammered Frank.

"I hope so, because you might be surprised, mister!" I winked at him, and he appeared thrown for a loop by my seductive innuendo.

The atmosphere that night was very romantic. Frank was in top form, too. We had very gradually become closer since the night of our long walk and our—as I still presumed, at least—first kiss. He walked me home that evening as usual, and I had finally resolved that it was time to invite him in upon this particular occasion. To that end, I had even arranged things with Mary so that I could have the house to myself that evening. Yet I still—as in all walks of my life—played my cards carefully. A lady had to take especial care of her reputation in those days, lest she be so much as even suspected of being what they called in New Orleans a *nymphe du pavé*. I was already compromised by my current profession as it was, appearing questionable in the eyes of some as a woman gambler employed by a gentlemen's casino. All the same, I found that by treading carefully, I came across to most as a "virtuous gambler" and thus given the benefit of the doubt.

Be that as it may, I did not yet know Frank well enough to "make a move" without fear of seeming unladylike. But thus far he had proven too much of a gentleman—or else just unexpectedly shy—to have progressed things sufficiently to my satisfaction. He wanted me though, of that I felt sure.

But I was now quite smitten—to use Will's earlier word of Frank's own feelings for me—although I still to this day cannot say exactly why. Perhaps I was drawn to the way he seemed an odd sort of rugged gentleman, possessing a unique combination of well-bred Georgia charm and a markedly (though equally endearing) natural backwoods wildness. I suppose his Cherokee half had much to do with the latter. Whatever it was, I found him irresistible.

As we walked home that evening, I described to Frank my recent discovery of a little bookstore on Main Street tucked unexpectedly between a barber shop and a saloon. I had gone into the barber shop to have my nails done by a manicurist employed there, and through the window saw a small sign advertising books. Upon entering, several books immediately caught my eye. Ever since arriving in Texas, I had longed for new reading material. Finding that bookstore was like stumbling upon a fertile oasis in the midst of a desert. One of the books was a collection of international poetry translations that included haiku by Basho, and so when we arrived at my door I asked Frank if he might care to come inside for a look at some of the poems. He did not disappoint. Before long, we were sipping wine on my Victorian loveseat and reading poetry out loud together.

I was pleased to find Frank a better reader than I had expected, given his at times "country" manner of speaking (which I had often suspected as being more for macho bravado than anything else, as he was very well-spoken when he wished to be). Hearing his voice reading verse aloud made me near explode with desire for him. He was wearing a black satin bow tie, which I soon found myself almost at unawares reaching up and untying. Then I tugged both ends toward me so that he had little recourse but to lower his handsome candle-lit face and kiss me. And that he did, with a sudden passion unlike any I had ever imagined.

Frank put down the book, and that night we read no more.

The next day as I walked to work with Mary, I felt a lilt in my step like I was walking on air. I had never felt such a warmth inside, certainly not after my first romantic experience (if it could even be called that) with Johnny. Of course, I was effectively still just a child then. This time, however, felt authentic and mature. It felt like love. For the very first time in my young life, I knew I was falling in love. And all I could think of was my desire to feel Frank's arms around me again as they were that previous night—and so repeated endlessly through an eternal succession of such nights.

There must have been some tell-tale glow about my look that day, though, judging from the knowing eye Mary gave me, along with the especially friendly salutations I received upon arrival at the University Club—first by the guards and then the old porter (who even gave the hint of a smile for once as I strode confidently inside). I glanced in the direction of the bar, where from his usual place, Frank reached up and gave a discreet half-tip of his hat. I nodded with a knowing smile.

When Mary and I took our places at the table, I in my chair behind the Faro box and she on her stool behind me, a group of men had already taken their seats with a number of others gathered round. (My particular table tended to draw a crowd of spectators each evening.) That night, everything started off smoothly as usual, as I shuffled the cards and prepared the layout. Just then, I heard a voice that I thought I recognized, though in an unpleasant sort of way. Mary must have seen him first, because I felt a tense touch from her hand on my shoulder.

When I looked up, I immediately knew who it was from the rebel flag tattoo on the back of his hand: a hand that now grasped the burned rim of his battle-scarred hat as he doffed it toward me. Then I saw the face I had hoped never to see again, this time with a mocking grin that displayed a bare gumline dotted with a few sparse and blackened teeth. When he spoke, his patronizing words were accented with a mean sarcasm only heightened by his southern drawl:

“Well now, if it ain’t for the feisty little hellcat from the Cosmopolitan Club and her hulking negress troll! When I heard about an angel workin’ here, I little reckoned that could ever mean you! I’ve had a hankering to see y’all again ever since that night.”

It was Mary who answered first. “Now look here, Mistah, we don’t want no trouble, hear?”

“Ain’t nothin’ to worry about here, leastways from me. That is, so long as we play by my rules. And I say we lay a little wager on you this time.” He pointed at me, and then added: “I win, and I get to take you home with me for a long ride in your sweet saddle.”

I said, “There’s only one set of rules here, and those are the rules of the University Club. You may either accept them or else depart, that is your choice.”

“Well, I’ll be goddamned! Don’t you give me no sass, little sister.”

“Please refrain from such language at this table. That is my particular rule, and I will not have anyone acting ugly.”

He laughed. "Well, I say fuck such rules! What do you say to that?"

"I say you're out of line, mister." This reply came from a familiar voice just behind me. It was Frank. The man's smile froze as he and Frank regarded each other carefully. Frank's pipe dangled from the side of his mouth, from which a cloud of smoke hid his expression. The other gamblers at the table abruptly got up and backed away while the crowd behind us quickly dispersed.

Frank said, "We don't cater to the likes of you." At that, the rebel ruffian slowly pushed back his chair and stood up. He leaned over the table and said, "Then cater to this." His tattooed hand now held and cocked a pistol, pointed directly at Frank just inches from his face. You could hear the proverbial pin drop in the room as the two men stood there staring each other down. The ruffian reached with his other hand in his pocket and extracted a plug of tobacco that he snagged with one of his pointy teeth. He chewed it deliberately for a moment before spitting it at Frank, upon the toe of whose boot the yellowish-brown mass found purchase.

"Mind the spittoon, mister," said Frank, pointing with his pipe to a shiny brass spittoon where it sat nearby. "There's one by every table." He flashed a wry smile at the other man, then lifted his pipe back to his lips and, much to everyone's amusement, blew a smoke ring that encircled the pistol's barrel before drifting into the man's face.

"I reckon," came the reply, "I mistook that silly hat of yours for the right place to spit. Sure makes you look a sissy. But maybe that's what them whores prefer, such like you got working here." He glanced at me and chuckled. Frank's smile sank into a frown as he drew the handkerchief from his front pocket and defied the gun in his face to stoop and wipe the spit from his boot. It struck me that he did this with his right hand. Meanwhile, he reached with his left hand behind his head to scratch his neck beneath the collar.

"I can tolerate most any kind of tomfoolery," said Frank. "Impertinence I simply cannot abide."

Quick as a hiccup, Frank drew out his Bowie knife from the hidden sheath under his jacket and slashed clean through the ruffian's gun hand at the wrist. The gun fired aimlessly as the now disembodied hand that grasped it fell with a thud onto the floor. The man gave a painful shriek and watched in horror as blood spurted from the stump where his hand had been and ran in rivulets about his feet and through the wooden floor panels.

With a quick backhand stroke, Frank now doubled back and stabbed him straight through the heart.

"Take that, you pigeon-livered ratbag!"

From the gathered onlookers came an incongruous mix of shocked gasps and muted laughter, while instinctively, I grabbed my card layout cloth and rushed over to staunch the poor fellow's bleeding with Mary's help. It was too late. He just stared at me with a look of such terrified disbelief that I almost pitied him as he gasped his last breath on the floor. I looked back to where Frank had stood, but he was gone.

PART III

Mystic Maud

9

"YOU MUST LEAVE TOWN, BROTHER."

Will's words, though they were halfway expected, still came as a sudden shock. Frank had just killed a man, after all, and the law regarding such matters was at that time (as ever in Texas) murky at best.

It was just after the incident with the ruffian, and I had found Frank in the lounge debating what to do next with Will. For my part, I downright begged him to take his chances before a jury with the legitimate plea of self-defense, but Will said the man Frank had felled was part of a renegade band of Confederates in San Antonio who would no doubt subscribe to vigilante justice regardless of the law. To my dismay, Frank agreed.

"With me on the run," Frank reasoned, "they'll be more likely just to come straight after me and leave you well enough alone. If I stay, you will be also in danger. I won't allow that."

Despite my protestations, Frank resolved to flee San Antonio under cover of darkness before daybreak.

His plan was to make for the network of forts the U.S. Army had set up along the western Texas frontier to protect settlers from Indian attacks and general lawlessness during the relentless push West.

He said, "There's a string of military posts up there, all of them hot spots for gambling in the local settlements. It's easy pickings for a gambler in all them saloons near the forts!"

"Then I am coming with you, sugar!" said I, with adamant resolve.

Frank smiled wistfully whilst shaking his head in the wrong direction. "No, shug, you are not. I will not have you put into any further danger on my account. You'll be safer here, for now. William Russell will look after you." He glanced at Will, who nodded his affirmation. I just breathed a loud sigh and looked away, trying to conceal the tears blurring my sight.

Word came later that night that the town marshal was on his way back from a visit to Austin and planned to arrest Frank as soon as he arrived early on the following day. So next morning before daybreak, I met Frank at the corral to see him off. Will was there with him, helping to prepare his saddlebags. The eastern sky already glimmered with long streaks of pinkish cloud as Frank prepared to mount Nell, a lovely chestnut mare and his fastest horse. Around his waist, he wore a bandolier belt stuffed with bullet cartridges, and he slung his trusty Winchester shotgun across his back attached to a strap. I knew right well where he had his blade.

He already had one foot in the stirrup when he

turned back and embraced me with a kiss. Will turned politely away to give us our moment. Frank looked at me with a tenderness then that I would never forget, and I felt him slip something made of cold round metal into my palm. I looked down and saw it was a silver locket.

Frank said, "A little something to remember me by." As he leapt into the saddle, he added: "I'm making for the Concho River valley. I hear tell they're building a new fort up there at the Army post along the river. Should be ripe for the picking!"

"I will find you," said I.

Frank nodded affirmatively. Then he reached in a saddlebag, took out a small pocket "gambler's pistol" and handed it to me.

He said, "Keep this handy wherever you are."

"But I don't..."

"Will can teach you."

He looked at Will, who nodded.

"And one more thing. I shall be traveling by an alias. Keep an ear out for the name Fogarty!"

He spurred Nell forward without another word. The horse gave a loud snort and swiftly galloped off down the road into the darkness. I just stood there with Will in silence, watching the horse and her rider disappear around the bend until the last sound of hoofbeats faded into the silence of the morning. Finally, I sighed with a sad half-smile to Will, turned away, and walked home in the crisp autumn air. Along the way, I stopped and opened the locket he had given me. Inside was a photograph of Frank, wearing his wonted Stetson hat.

10

It was not long after the marshal's return that "Wanted" signs appeared bearing Frank's image. The locket he gave me now hung from my favorite gold necklace as a pendant, and upon passing such posters on the street, I would invariably reach up and grasp it with a knowing smile before instinctively speeding up my pace. But there were no signs of the posse that Frank had feared. Indeed, in conversations that I overheard about the matter, the general consensus about town concerning the ruffian's death appeared to be that "it needed to be done." I nevertheless resolved to bide my time for a while so as to deter any suspicion if I were to depart suddenly, as I had become somewhat notorious about town as a "lady gambler" (as had, alas, my somewhat indiscreet affinity for Frank). My hope was that once I deemed sufficient time had passed since his departure, I might eventually succeed in finding Frank somewhere along the Texas frontier. Yet now I lived each day in dread of hearing news of his capture.

Mary, however, would have none of it. She was distraught at the suggestion of leaving San Antonio, where her newfound freedom had led to close friendships and a sense of real community for the first time in her life. She, therefore, put her foot down at any talk of leaving.

She said, "But I can't leave now, Miss Carlotta! I got friends here, and people to help!"

"How can I go without you, Mary? After all we've been through together. I'm lost without you!"

Mary smiled reassuringly. "You stronger than you think, child! And the road ahead is all your own now to follow."

"Then I'm leaving all this to you," I replied, trying to stifle my tears.

"Leaving what, Miss Carlotta?"

"Why, this house, Mary! And everything in it I can't take with me. Which is most everything."

Mary appeared overwhelmed with emotion. She shook her head no at first but saw my resolve.

"Lawsamercy, honey! God bless you, Miss Carlotta."

She embraced me tearfully, as I stared over her broad shoulder and cried too, wondering if she was yet another loved one I might never see again. I was devastated at the thought of departing without my constant companion (as well as protector) throughout all of our many adventures together since my childhood.

I spent the next several weeks biding my time while continuing to deal cards at the Club, though my heart was full of anguish, and it was all I could do to focus on the task at hand. I wanted nothing more than to board the next stagecoach out of town, yet something kept holding me back. I reckon it was a combination of fear of the unknown and doubt as to the extent of my own inner strength—despite that which I always sought outwardly to portray. My winnings, however, began to display a marked decline during that time.

One evening, Will called me into the reception

room for a talk.

"If you still mean to go through with your plan," he said, "then you had best go soon. The cold weather's coming on when the roads west and north will be difficult."

This was all the catalyst I needed to spur me finally to action, and now I discreetly began my preparations for the journey. But if I still had any unresolved doubts about leaving, a sudden development brought a new sense of heightened urgency.

One day soon afterward, a letter arrived for me at the University Club in a hand I had almost forgotten. The letter was postmarked from New Orleans, and the moment I received it from the porter, I tore it open with a sense of sudden dread.

My dearest Carlotta,

> I write this with the odd sense of hopeful trepidation one feels upon resurfacing, like the prodigal son, after a long and inexcusable absence. Please know, however, that my truancy was through no fault of my own, in that I was detained during the war (and for some time following) due to an unfortunate occurrence that I shall make known to you in due course. All that concerns you at present is that I am now at liberty to fulfill our long-held promise of reuniting in San Antonio, where I have learned here in New Orleans that you have indeed finally reached. Your reputation quite precedes you! I so dearly long to see you once again, and to travel together West just as we once planned in Detroit. How long ago that seems now! To that end, I am departing New Orleans forthwith and should

arrive in San Antonio very soon after this letter finds its place in your lovely hands.

Yours most affectionately,

Johnny

I sat abruptly back and stared at the letter in disbelief, murmuring to myself aloud: "Johnny! I thought by now that you surely must be dead!"

I rushed home panic-stricken and spent the rest of the afternoon hastily stuffing my many fine garments into my trunk. It was a Tuesday, and I knew that the western stagecoach departed San Antonio every Wednesday morning promptly at eight o'clock. I sent Mary to the Club to inform Will of my plans, and he duly returned word that he would arrive at seven with a buggy for transport to the stage station at Alamo Plaza.

And that is how I found myself on a bright and chilly November morning at the side entrance of the Menger Hotel, boarding a stagecoach to the yonder unknown. Although I had taken every precaution to keep my departure quiet, I still looked around nervously for fear of being followed—and of seeing Johnny. Will helped the stage driver load my rather hefty trunk onto the leather-covered luggage boot at the back, and before climbing in, I quietly hugged Will.

He said, "Good luck, Angel! Give my love to Frank when you find him."

"Of that you may be sure!" I turned to Mary, and we tearfully embraced.

I said, "I'll miss you, my old friend."

"You just take good care of yourself, honey!"

I could think of nothing more to say, so I took the driver's extended hand and stepped up into the coach. Moments later, I heard the whip crack over the four-horse team and felt the carriage lurch forward with creaking wheels, carrying me to God only knew what adventures (or perhaps misadventures) lay ahead.

As I watched Mary and Will waving at me until they and the Alamo vanished around a bend, I felt a sudden pang of dread.

II

FOUR OTHER PASSENGERS were on the venerable old Concord stagecoach as it rolled down the dusty road west like a giant teacup on wheels. My traveling companions from San Antonio consisted of a middle-aged, monocle-wearing doctor and his newlywed young wife. I was pleased to hear the doctor had likewise the destination of the frontier forts (as I had been warned to expect little to nothing in the way of medicine thereabouts), despite his clearly being as green at his profession as an unripe tomato still on the vine. Apart from that, there was only the driver above, along with—riding "shotgun" next to him—the messenger overseeing the mail sacks (who also carried a heavy Sharps rifle and served as lookout for such myriad perils along the way as Indians and the notorious bands of highwaymen). Judging from the looks of my fellow travelers, any such dangers as thieves and attacking Indians were bound to be poorly met, and I could only pray silently to myself for safe passage.

The road we were to follow was the pre-war San Antonio-San Diego mail route, before detouring northwest along the Austin-Fredericksburg stage line and finally to Fort Chadbourne, where it joined the old "Butterfield" Overland Mail Company route west to El Paso and from thence to Santa Fe and finally California. I was told that if the roads were in a passable state (depending upon decently dry weather), we could make around sixty miles a day and arrive at my destination within the week. That, of course, proved wishful thinking. (And any significant rain could make various rivers along the way impassable for days or even weeks on end.) The journey's first leg to Austin was a good eighty miles, which could be made as quickly as a day and a half in good weather, or up to a week if wet. If I had any second thoughts, it was soon too late to turn back, as before long San Antonio was far behind us while the coach rolled on the rest of that day without stopping through the night.

I later read the late Mr. Clemens' description of Concord coach travel as "an imposing cradle on wheels." Well, all I know is if this was his idea of feeling cradled, then I would hate to go roughing it with Sam Clemens! Trying to sleep that first night was akin to getting tossed about on a steamship in rough waters as it swayed from side to side. The red upholstered seats were rather worn and uncomfortable, and I spent most of the night huddled in my corner by the drawn curtain, occasionally peering out into the darkness. There was a full moon, and from its light, I could make out a faint line of hills shimmering in the distance. By the time we reached our first stop later that first day, I felt dashed as a deviled egg. I no doubt looked it, too, but there was no mirror to be had. Certainly not at the decrepit stop (the first of many such stage stands along the way, located at approximate ten-mile intervals though still too few and far between for my liking) where we finally alighted after many miles of stagecoaching through hill country, and where there was naught but an old well and a filthy lean-to with a hole in the ground for an outhouse. Here we were provided a meal consisting of tough venison, baked Irish potatoes, and cold cornbread. The only saving grace was a glass of refreshingly cool sweet milk. Certainly far from ideal! "When I was at home, I was in a better place, but travelers must be content."

Fortunately, the weather stayed dry, and by the end of the next day we reached the capital city of Austin, where we lodged the night at an inn for a much-needed respite to soothe my aching bones. We departed at sunrise after a delicious breakfast of bacon and eggs, buttered grits, hot cakes, and coffee. (That was the last decent meal to be had for some days). The tolerable weather continued to hold, and I enjoyed the next stage of the trip somewhat better now after a proper rest, feeling refreshed and better accustomed to the rigors of long-distance stage travel.

Our stagecoach also had a new driver and a fresh team of horses–two beautiful galloping spans who launched us swiftly forward out of Austin in a cloud of dust. Two new travelers also now joined us: a couple of well-dressed "whiskey drummers" planning to peddle their "liquid gold" (as one of them put it) as the top commodity in the frontier settlements.

My fellow passengers did not say much and generally just chatted amongst themselves whenever they did speak. The salesmen sitting together across from me talked mostly about business, the doctor and his wife mostly about the landscape–and the rather striking flora and fauna spotted along the way. The young wife–Emily–sat next to me in the middle between the doctor and myself, and I would sometimes engage her in talk of no more consequence than could be respectfully overheard by all.

To stave off boredom, I filled much of the time scribbling in a diary. I always thought at such times about Frank, when I often felt such a terrible longing that I would stare for hours out the window, watching the landscape roll by. But in my mind's eye, I was far away, wondering where he was and what he was doing. And if he were safe.

When the others appeared distracted with their own affairs, I would sometimes steal a glance at Frank's picture in the locket he gave me. On one such occasion, my eyes looked up to meet those of Emily's next to me, glancing likewise at the picture before I quickly snapped shut the locket, but she gave me a knowing look with a quick smile and turned back to her husband.

As a general rule in those days, inquisitiveness was severely frowned upon, especially along the frontier. One would rarely, if ever, be asked personal details such as one's business or place of origin, much less one's name. But if conversation were ever to lead unavoidably in that direction, you were free to provide whatever personal story (and name) you wished. In consequence, the art of telling tall tales about oneself became somewhat of a fashion. Hence also the skepticism and immediate distrust which greeted the arrival of any new stranger to a frontier settlement.

For my part, as I certainly must, of necessity, travel "incognito," I settled upon the name of "Maud" after a favorite aunt back home. The story I concocted was that I hailed from New Orleans—hence explaining my particular wardrobe—where I came from an aristocratic family who had lost everything during the recent "War between the States." Having been taught gambling by my father (who had died fighting in the late war), I was heading West in hopes of earning money to send back home to help my invalid mother put my younger sister through school. If further pressed, I would also admit to fleeing a violent drunk of a husband who had once threatened to kill me, but to whom I nevertheless felt a religious obligation to remain faithful by virtue of my wedding vows. (This last detail, I hoped, might suffice to ward off trouble down the road.) Such was my story, and I was pleased that it partly at least smacked of the truth.

Throughout the rest of the long journey, there was seldom any further interaction with my fellow travelers beyond the most mundane of superficial small talk. But at one point, the doctor spoke to me directly when he observed my keen interest in a certain spectacle upon the road. We had not yet progressed very far from Austin when we stopped briefly to allow the passing upon either side of a large regiment of soldiers that had overtaken us. This in itself was nothing peculiar, as there was much movement of troops in those days en route to fortify the frontier garrisons against the Indians during the inexorable push to settle the West. Yet these soldiers were remarkably different in that the entire cavalry regiment was colored.

"They're known as the Buffalo Soldiers," remarked the doctor, observing my intrigued expression.

I asked, "Why might that be?"

"It is what the Indians call them, on account of their valiant ferocity in battle. Quite the compliment, too, as the Indians hold few things higher in reverence than the buffalo."

"But who are they?"

"Congress created these colored regiments after the war to help protect settlers on the frontier."

"Protect them from what?"

The doctor chuckled. "Why, from all the Indians, cattle rustlers, and bandits that plague the land out here. And we'd best hope there's a regiment of these soldiers around if we happen to encounter any of those!"

His wife and I exchanged an alarmed look at hearing this and looked outside nervously as we heard the driver's whip crack, and our stagecoach moved forward again.

I discovered much more later about how in those days when the Texas Rangers had yet to be recommissioned following the War, the "Buffalo Soldiers" of the 9th Cavalry were tasked to secure the roads to the forts. (They were also later used by the U.S. government to help enforce the removal of the native Americans from their original homelands to the reservations, the irony of which did not escape me.)

Yet now, I suddenly felt a comforting sense of reassurance as I watched these soldiers. When one of them happened to glance in our direction as they passed, I gave a quick wave of my hand in hopes of conveying a signal of gratitude. The young man touched his dark hat with its crossed saber insignia and nodded with a fulsome smile before spurring his horse forward past the coach.

We soon came to the Colorado River, which—thanks to the recent dry weather—was lower than usual for the time of year. An old wartime pontoon bridge was still in use there, and the driver politely requested us to step out of the coach to lighten the load in hopes of transporting it across without mishap. We duly obliged, and I found myself walking somewhat precariously across the floating span as it bobbed up and down beneath the combined weight of people, horses, and our stagecoach. Upon reaching the further bank, I had to sit for a few moments to counter a short spell of dizziness such as I had not felt since first boarding the steamship in Detroit.

After that, we made good time through the rolling, hilly landscape over the next several days. I took pleasure in watching the landscape transform as we traversed it across the miles— though I wished it were earlier in the year when the many fabled Texas wildflowers were still in bloom. As it was, about the only such flowers to be seen among the sagebrush were the purple prairie verbena and a few other perennials, including yellow cutleaf daisies scattered among throngs of cactus and mesquite. The scenery was still beautiful, especially when we rode through tangled wildwoods or atop large hillsides with fine vistas of all the country round. We passed through prairie land dotted with groves of live oak, cypress, hickory, juniper, and even occasional pecan trees—beneath whose thick branches, at one stop, I gathered sufficient pecans for a future pie or two.

Eventually, we reached Fredericksburg in the heart of Texas Hill Country. The small town on the Pedernales River, originally founded earlier in the century by German settlers, has hence become known for its "Lager" and beer gardens. After locating the famous Nimitz Hotel, we stayed for a most enjoyable night that everyone knew was the last such vestige of "civilization" (including a proper hot bath!) before reaching the frontier forts. In the dining room, there was a fine piano in the corner, and I drew quite a grateful crowd when I proceeded to play a Beethoven sonata after dinner that evening.

The next day we rode almost thirty miles, crossing over the mountains I had previously noted from a distance. From Fredericksburg, our route joined with the military road to the western posts on which numerous military units were moving among the various forts. We stopped to rest at a stage station called Loyal Valley, where there was a small store run by a young German couple. Soon after that, we had to ford a couple of streams. The first was shallow and rocky, and we were able to get across without too much trouble. The second, however, which our lookout named Frog Pond Creek, was deeper, and our new stage driver (not nearly as polite as the first one) ordered us all off the coach again, this time to wade through the water on our own accord behind the stagecoach. At one point, the coach became stuck in the midst of the stream with one of its wheels apparently wedged between rocks, and the two drummers were enlisted in joining with the driver and messenger to help it along. By the time I got back on the coach, the lower half of my dress was soaked, and it was all I could do later to scrub out all the mud. The further bank took us across a flat plain dotted with cactus and mesquite, and on a hill in the distance, I saw what remained of an old, long-deserted fort.

Our next stop was at Peg Leg Station, a relay post on the old Overland Mail Company stage line named for a soldier who once had his leg blown off by a cannonball. The adobe brick station house was, like most in those parts, built up on a high rise where it had a good view in all directions. I observed that its gateway and all of its windows were barred.

After that, we went through a patch of deep woods before emerging out onto the prairie again, where I was utterly bemused at the sight of what looked at first like hundreds of oversized squirrels chasing one other about the plain. The doctor called them "prairie dogs" and noted the many holes dotting the fields that he said were considered a pesky nuisance by local ranchers. I nevertheless found the little critters delightful to watch as they piped their high-pitched barks at us before darting into their holes as we passed by. These were not the only intriguing wildlife to be seen on the prairies and arroyos we crossed, as we also observed wild turkeys and doves, swooping hawks, and even several herds of antelope. I was disappointed in one thing, though: I had sorely wished finally to see the roaming herds of buffalo I had heard so much about since I was little whenever folk told stories of the frontier. But the driver said they tended to graze on the plains farther to the west at that time of year.

We continued along the rest of that day until reaching the stage stop at Coglin's Ranch. Here we had a good rest, along with a satisfying meal comprised of sweet potatoes, boiled cabbage, and antelope steaks. I hesitated at first over the latter, but my adventurous streak got the better of me and—upon putting out of mind the graceful creatures seen just earlier that day grazing upon the prairie—found the meat tender and delectable.

The following morning we departed after a scrumptious breakfast of rabbit and cheese, traveling apace until reaching in late afternoon a small creek at Kickapoo Springs. The weather was unseasonably warm, and the parched horses plunged eagerly into the water to drink their fill while the driver and messenger filled our nearly empty kegs. Noticing the anxious countenance on our driver's face, I inquired if something were not amiss.

"These are dangerous parts," he said, shaking his head. "This is an old Injun pass, and they're known to muster here sometimes before going off on raids. Especially now after the soldiers done come and built up those new forts and started slaughtering all the buffalo. Them Injuns hereabouts are all stirred up like a hive of bees!"

The messenger chimed in angrily. "The government's trying to force them out of their native lands and onto the reservations, to make way for settlers. They ain't too partial to travelers, neither. A band of Kiowa warriors attacked a stage that come through this way a while back. Scalped everyone aboard! Hence those graves over yonder."

He gestured to a shady spot beneath an oak by the stream. There, we found several small stones with the letters "R.I.P." carved crudely onto each. As I stared at them, I wondered about the unfortunate travelers lying there in shallow graves and could only hope the end they met there had been one without prolonged pain or torture.

I instinctively reached up and pulled at a lock of my hair.

"Heavens!" I exclaimed. "I shudder to think what a trophy a red-headed scalp like mine would make!"

Now the driver exhorted us to climb back aboard, which I, for one, could not do quickly enough after what

I had just heard. But then, as if bearing witness to the driver's tale, I saw something glinting in the shallow water and reached down to pick it up. It was an arrowhead and I jerked back my finger in surprise when the sharp tip pricked me. I decided to keep it as a souvenir from the trip, whilst trying hard not to surmise for what purpose the arrow had once been used. As if reading my mind, the good doctor standing nearby sought to reassure me.

"They won't attack us once we're closer to the new forts. They know full well they'll be tracked down by soldiers and their whole camp severely punished if they do!"

I nodded doubtfully in reply as I accepted his hand in helping me back up and into the coach, where I shared a nervous glance with Emily. Despite the doctor's words, everyone seemed noticeably uneasy. I also had the uncomfortable feeling we were being watched as our stage ambled along the trail, though maybe this was just my imagination getting the best of me again.

The temperature dropped quickly that night as we climbed up into the hills and high dales through a dense thicket of chaparral, and there were snow flurries by the next morning. I huddled beneath a thin and scratchy wool blanket inside the coach and later awoke with a start when the driver abruptly applied the stagecoach brakes, locking its wheels to help our safe passage downhill.

The driver guessed that, with luck, we should reach Fort Chadbourne—another old "Butterfield" stage station–later that morning, and he was not mistaken. We rolled into the fort early that afternoon, where the first things I noticed were the "mountain howitzer" cannons along the road. With those ominous barrels propped between their many-spoked wagon wheels, they looked like gigantic walking sticks glaring at us as we passed.

The fort itself was a hubbub of activity, with soldiers busily loading wagons and hauling supplies.

"They're moving out," commented one of the drummers.

"Where to?" I asked.

"The U.S. Army post at Concho," answered the doctor. "This old fort is being decommissioned due to water and supply shortages here. They're moving to the new one being built along the Concho River. I am to be the fort doctor there!" He smiled at Emily.

The doctor explained that in order to get to the new fort at the Concho post, we would have to arrange transport with troops making their way in that direction. I was glad they were making that trip with me, too, as I could only imagine the soldiers' reaction if a lady with my looks suddenly appeared in their midst seeking conveyance with them directly to their post. Fortunately, the doctor knew the ranking officer, who found transport for us on a battered and dusty old "celerity wagon" or mud wagon (a sort of improvised stagecoach) with a four-mule team. With the help of the two drummers, we managed with some difficulty to squeeze our luggage onto the wagon's boot (the doctor and Emily having brought "everything but the kitchen sink" with them). Before leaving, I bid farewell to the drummers, who, as traveling salesmen, sought to ply their wares at a new post further northeast on the Clear Fork of the Brazos River called Camp Wilson.

The three of us then climbed aboard along with a lookout and driver. With a lash from the whip, the wagon lurched forward with a jolt for the bumpy trip southwards to the Concho River valley.

12

BY AND BY, we came after around thirty miles of surprisingly swift travel (the speed of our mules much belied their size) to the Concho River. The pontoon bridge there had washed away during a recent flood, and we were forced to ford the river with great care. This proved a close call, too, as the troop of distant rumbling storm clouds that had threatened rain all day finally broke that evening in a driving "Blue Norther"—bringing with it a flash flood that rendered the river treacherously impassable for some weeks after that. But the mules, being used to crossing by bridge, proved stubborn when it came to fording the river. The driver and messenger labored with much travail to lead them across. Once again, we passengers were ordered perforce to "abandon ship" and wade through the water as best we could. At last, we reached the farther bank with the wagon, where the mules again refused to budge.

They say in Texas, you just need to unharness a mule and let him have a good roll in the dirt, and then he will continue happily for many miles. (Our driver had also said mules could sniff out Indians from miles away and give warning with a peculiar bray they have.) As with most such tales that Texans will tell you, I gave this little credence. But eventually–and after much coaxing–the mules finally took off with a trot toward my long-awaited destination.

After being further jostled over several more miles in the creaky old mud wagon, it was with sore limbs and an aching head that I greeted the sight of early evening campfires ahead. A new U.S. Army fort was under construction on the banks where the Concho and North Concho rivers met. (It was then still named Camp Kelly, soon to be called Fort Concho.) When we arrived there, the grassy parade ground was teeming with activity. There was something of a festive atmosphere afoot around the temporary barracks for the troops of infantrymen and cavalry posted there, including bonfires with large turkeys roasting on spits.

Emily pointed excitedly at the celebration. "What's the occasion, I wonder?"

The doctor smiled. "Thanksgiving, my dear!"

This caught me by surprise as well. "Thanksgiving already? Good heavens, I'd lost track of the time!"

Once again, the doctor and Emily were warmly greeted by the new fort's acting commanding officer. He approached our coach on horseback as we rolled into the camp, where they were to receive lodging at a primitive post hospital still under construction. I noticed Emily's look of dismay as she quickly surveyed her new home. Upon the officer's noticing me with a curious look, the doctor made to introduce me.

"And may I present ... forgive me, but what shall I call you, miss?"

I smiled and said: "You may call me Maud."

"Very well, then. Allow me to present Miss Maud."

At this, the officer tipped his hat and politely took my hand. "A pleasure to make your acquaintance, miss. Captain George Gibson Huntt, Fourth U.S. Cavalry, at your service."

"The pleasure is mine, Captain! If you will, where might I find decent lodging hereabouts?"

He gave me a rather questioning look before instructing the driver to take me "Over the River," as it was then referred to among soldiers in the camp. (I would later learn that the "Over the River" inhabitants themselves referred to their abode as "Across the River.")

"There's just one hotel over yonder," said the captain. "It is run by an Englishman named Veck. That and just about everything else over the river. He and his wife came out here a few months back and built a store with a saloon and a bank. And that hotel. He is a decent enough fellow, it seems." The captain winked at me and added: "But just one look at you, and I reckon he'll try putting you to good use in the little house above that saloon, if you take my meaning."

This last remark provoked lewd laughter amongst the soldiers standing by, though the doctor frowned with an embarrassed cough, and Emily blushed. She touched my arm and looked at me concernedly, entreating: "You take good care of yourself!"

All of this hardly concerned me at that moment. I was bursting with anxiety to visit that very saloon myself–where I could only pray I would find Frank waiting for me. Filled with a sudden feeling of hope, I instinctively took the locket in my hand and grasped it tightly.

It was some time yet before the tiny hamlet "Across the River" would be ultimately rechristened as San Angela (now Angelo) after the wife of a local landowner. But for now, it was nothing more than a drab hodge-podge of shabby buildings consisting of the aforesaid store, saloon, hotel, and a crude jail constructed with rotting logs. There were also a number of small adobe houses (more like huts) farther down the road.

It was just after dark when the mules came to a halt in front of a long wooden building that looked rather like a large shed. The entrance was lit with a single lantern, above which I could dimly see a sign that read "W.S. Veck's Store & Saloon." A loud din of voices sounded from somewhere in the back, which I later discovered was the saloon behind the store itself. There was nobody to be seen on the front porch or just within the entrance, but after unloading my trunk from the wagon boot and setting it down on the porch, the driver pointed to a counter inside.

"Just ring that bell on the counter, and someone should come out directly." Then, after a quick tip of his hat, he jumped again aboard the wagon and turned the mules around back toward camp. I did as he said and rang the handbell. While I waited, I took a good look around the store, which—apart from a meager collection of basic goods such as coffee, flour, and kegs of gunpowder—consisted mostly of buffalo hides. There appeared to be thousands of the stretched hides stacked up in every possible space awaiting shipment, along with an almost overwhelming stench.

Before too long, a balding man with a scraggly gray beard who looked to be around sixty appeared from a room in the back, followed by an attractive young woman I presumed his daughter before observing their matching rings.

I said, "Mr.—and Mrs.—Veck, I presume?"

"The same! And how may I help you, my dear?" He gave me a mischievous wink. I noticed with some discomfort his roving eyes taking unwelcome note of my person.

"I was told you have a hotel here, and I would like a room, please."

"I am terribly sorry, miss, but the hotel is full this evening. We have been overrun with skinners!" He gestured to the huge stacks of buffalo hides lining the floors.

"That explains the awful stench here, I'm afraid," he continued. "But not to worry, I have a vacant house where you may lodge at quite a reasonable rate."

"Much obliged to you."

"Just wait here a moment while I bring the buggy round."

I noticed Mrs. Veck observing me carefully during these proceedings, and she shot me a wary look of warning before vanishing into the back room. I had little other recourse but to accept, what with not knowing the way in the dark and being encumbered with luggage.

I was relieved to get outside and breathe the fresh air again. As we rode down the dark street in his lantern-lit buggy drawn by a single mule, Mr. Veck proved unreservedly direct in his discourse, which he spoke in a thick Cockney accent. When we passed a tall building with a sign that read "Hotel Concho" over the entrance, he turned and looked back at me curiously.

"May I ask, what brings such a charming young lady as yourself to a lonely outpost like this?"

After telling him my aforementioned story concocted for just such occasions, I added: "I have learned that a cousin of mine has come to these parts, and I aim to find him. A gentleman by the name of Fogarty. Do you know him?"

Mr. Veck reined in the mule and brought the buggy to a stop in front of the small house that was to be my lodging. "Fogarty ..." he repeated thoughtfully. "Now, that does ring a bell. Ah, yes, there was a gentleman by that name here several weeks ago. A tall fellow with a funny hat. Mike Fogarty, he called himself. Stayed for a time in the hotel."

I tried to subdue my sudden excitement.

"Is he still here?"

"That I do not rightly know. I haven't seen him in

some time. But Chess might know."

"Chess?"

"The barkeep at my saloon."

I impulsively looked behind the buggy, half inclined to jump off and run back up the road to the saloon. As if reading my thoughts, Mr. Veck added:

"Best wait till morning, my dear. The Concho Saloon is no place for a lady after dark. Unless ...," he said with another suggestive wink, as he got out and unloaded my trunk from the buggy.

"Unless?" I asked, anxiously following him as he carried my trunk to the door.

Mr. Veck set the trunk down at the entrance. "Unless you prefer to work after dark, if you take my meaning? I should be delighted to offer you employment of a particular kind at my saloon. Very profitable in these parts too, I assure you, if ..."

"You quite mistake me, Mr. Veck," I interjected, before enlightening him in no uncertain terms of the insulting nature of his suggestion.

"I am a lady of class and good breeding," I insisted, "and do not take kindly to such lewd and ungentlemanly assumptions."

Mr. Veck appeared taken aback. "Then I must crave your forgiveness, I did not mean to..."

"I am, however, much adept at employment of a much different sort that I hope may interest you." I took from my purse a deck of cards and expertly shuffled it before his eyes.

"A lady who can ply the pasteboards," he said thoughtfully. "Yes, that should do very well for us in the saloon!"

He unlocked the door and lit the lone lamp inside, where I was shocked at what I saw. The place that was to be my temporary home in "Across the River" was the poorest excuse for a "house" I had ever seen. It was no more than a wretched little hovel of a hut: a tiny adobe structure whose once white walls were covered in dust from the dirt floor. There was naught in it but some tin plates and cooking utensils on a small table and an iron stove with a pile of kindling tucked in a corner to serve both for cooking and for warmth. There was also a rusty old chamber pot by the little cot serving for a bed, upon which was spread a raggedy quilt. I spotted numerous chinks in the adobe walls that, in places, had been shoddily daubed with mud in a futile attempt to stifle the chill draft.

Once Mr. Veck had left me alone there, I found myself weeping for no particular reason, other than in questioning how I had let my life come to such a sorry pass. It was at such times that I especially missed Mary, with her true friendship conjoined with her protective eye that made me feel safe.

It was Thanksgiving Day, and I felt like the loneliest person in the world.

13

THE FOLLOWING AFTERNOON, I attracted the usual attention upon strutting into the saloon as if I owned it, and I was acutely aware of all eyes following my every movement. The saloon was probably the most sordid I had seen to date. The smoke that filled it was that of cheap tobacco with the harshest of scents, and the only other women there were likewise of the cheapest sort, wearing red ruffled skirts and feather headpieces. Lest I be mistaken for one of them, I had insisted that Mr. Veck be there to introduce me as his new poker dealer and show me to my table. It did not take long for me to amass a crowd, which consisted of mostly young greenhorns from the Army camp (where gambling was illegal) who seemed happy to be relieved of their meager pay for just a few minutes in my company. (The ladies otherwise in Mr. Veck's employment seemed none too pleased with this new competition for the local boys' time—and money—and I took extra care to avoid them.)

The greatest challenge was in trying to hide my deep anxiety that first day over failing to find Frank there. Mr. Veck had told me that the person to ask would be the young bartender named Chess, and I waited patiently for a quiet moment to approach the bar. I had taken Frank's picture out of the locket so as not to seem too conspicuous when I described him as my "cousin" and showed it to Chess. The young man scrutinized it for a few moments, before a look of recognition appeared on his face.

He said, "Yeah, I remember the gentleman! Mike Fogarty, he called himself. One helluva gambler, too, I reckon."

Trying to contain my excitement, I replied: "That is excellent news. And is he ... Mike ... still hereabouts?"

To my great dismay, he shook his head in the wrong direction. "No, miss, he left a couple of weeks back."

"Did he say where he was going?"

"No...wait, yes...Yes, he did! He said he'd heard stories of richer pickings at Jacksboro, up near that new post called Fort Richardson. And that if anyone was to ask after him, that's where he might be found."

I thanked Chess and, much to his surprise and delight, discreetly downed a shot of whiskey before returning to my table. I lost the next few rounds of poker that day, being so distracted. I had finally heard news of Frank, which was something at least. But he was still elsewhere, and now I needed to study what to do next.

With the news of Frank's earlier departure, I decided after thinking on it all night that my sojourn at Concho must be brief. However, I had to replenish my coffers at that point before venturing forth upon further (and quite unexpected) travels. I had worried about losing my table in the saloon once Mr. Veck learned of my initial losses, but on the following day I made short order of recouping them (and then some), and he was well pleased. It would be several more weeks before my winnings were sufficient to provide traveling money for the trip to Jacksboro.

In the meantime, the little community of "Across the River" ran rife with rumors about me, and it was all I could do just to keep to myself without molestation, socially and otherwise. (Some of the gossip I overheard hit uncomfortably near to the truth, too: that I was waiting for—or maybe hunting for—a man, maybe even an outlaw on the lam.) The inhabitants there consisted of a fine collection of riffraff, including cowhands from the local ranches, buffalo hunters, wayward cattle drovers, and general no-good drifters of every possible description. There was also no law yet to be found there outside the camp, apart from the occasional act of vigilante justice, and the dilapidated jail was mostly just for show. Chess told me that Mrs. Veck liked to say, "The law here is your pistol, and you should carry as many as you can pack!" I was sure glad I had the pocket "gambler's pistol" Frank gave me before he left—and that Will had taught me to use. I almost had to use it a time or two, especially when I was sometimes accused of being a "cheat"—most men just could not fathom a woman who wasn't "crooked" being able to win at cards. For that reason especially, I took to wearing boots that offered a convenient hiding place for the nifty little gun.

The local rabble soon had a name of their own for me too, inspired by speculation surrounding my mysterious ways and provenance: "Mystic Maud," they dubbed me, which suited me just fine for a local cognomen (whatever they might really have meant by it). I hear the moniker of Mystic Maud is still recalled in the tales of those parts even now!

But truth be told, I could not get away fast enough from that place and determined to do so by Christmas. And it was indeed Christmas Eve before I finally started the trek to Jacksboro, about a hundred fifty miles northeast. Once again, if I had had any second thoughts about leaving, they were quickly dispelled by a bit of unexpected news from San Antonio. Will promised to communicate if there was any news of consequence—I had confided to him about Johnny Golden—and sure enough, a letter addressed simply to "Maud" arrived at the fort the day before I was to leave. (Will had assumed, quite rightly, that I would not be unknown to the men around camp by that time.) The envelope also bore the ominous word "Urgent," so that I guessed before perusing the letter inside what it might portend.

I guessed rightly: Johnny Golden had heard gossip of my passage north, and he was now in hot pursuit!

PART IV

"Lotta Dinero"

14

I LEFT WITHOUT SAYING A WORD to anyone apart from Chess, whom I had found quite congenial and deemed sufficiently trustworthy to know my intentions. With his help, I arranged conveyance back across the river to camp, where I could board the mail stage that provided service to the various posts further north. I simply left the key behind on the table in my ramshackle hut of a house—along with payment for the final week and a terse note for Mr. Veck to the effect that news had arrived from home that necessitated my immediate departure.

If the recent rains had not stopped when they did, I would have been in a fine fix indeed, being stuck in "Across the River" to dread the inevitable arrival of Johnny any day and the consequent (and perhaps fatal) disruption of all my hopes. The Concho River was still treacherously high as it was, but the pontoon bridge had withstood the flooding, and I arrived upon the further bank safe and dry. There I rescued from the mud a lovely shell or "conch" (hence the river's very name, with its freshwater mussels famous for their pink pearls).

Despite the chilly air, there was a flurry of excitement when I arrived at the fort later that morning. Soldiers from different companies were out on the parade grounds amidst the enlisted men's barracks, engaging in a fascinating activity. They called it "Base Ball," and it was a mighty fine sight to see them running the "bases" upon the cracking echo of bat against ball. It was a far cry from the game as it is played now in those fancy ballparks back East, but there was something so raw and exhilarating about the way those soldiers were playing it that day that I was hard-pressed to turn away and board the waiting stage. That was a sight I have always recalled with great relish.

It was a bright sunny morning as our mule team sauntered along toward the Twin Mountains in the distance and past the quarries from which the limestone was mined for constructing the barracks and other buildings at Fort Concho. This time I was the lone passenger in the stagecoach, otherwise manned as usual, with a driver and the "shotgun messenger" in charge of safe delivery of the mail and carrying across his lap a Spencer carbine shotgun. I should not have felt particularly safe by this arrangement, yet somehow I did. I had become rather adept at my capacity to read people—especially men—to "find the mind's construction in the face," and quickly concluded as we "celebrated" Christmas that evening singing carols (with harmonica accompaniment!) by the campfire that I had nothing to fear from these two old cowboys escorting me through the Texas wilderness. A trip that was largely uneventful, if not even something enjoyable—apart, of course, from the constant fear of a violent Indian attack or robbery.

But I have often recalled with nostalgia those days traveling alone, contemplating naught but the steady clop of the mules' hooves and the creak of the wagon wheels over gravel (counterpointed with the reassuring chatter of the men above discussing the fortunes to be made out West through cattle and gold). And, at long last, I saw a much longed-for sight: herds of free-roaming bison on the plains, as far as the eye could see. It was a vision I often recall now with sadness, as with their ultimate passing from the frontier plains, so went the true spirit of the Old West itself.

The nights, however, were a very different story, spent huddled under thin blankets shivering and trying to avoid the frigid draft whistling through the coach as I struggled to catch some sleep. Often I just crouched, listening to the spooky hooting of owls intermingled with the braying of coyotes. At such times, how I yearned to be back in my house in San Antonio, my feet propped up on a settle with Frank by my side on the old loveseat by the warm hearth. Fortunately, at each stop, there was a chance to warm my cold bones by the campfire before freezing to death. I just hoped not to catch pneumonia by the journey's end.

By and by, one clear but cold evening at sunset, we finally crossed the bridge over Lost Creek leading into the small town of Jacksboro. Knowing Johnny was on my trail, I knew I had best leave the name "Maud" behind at Fort Concho and find a new alias—one which would soon present itself courtesy of a random encounter.

15

JACKSBORO WAS A SOMEWHAT NEW township with a local population of around three hundred citizens, having been settled in the 1850s by pioneers drawn by Texas land offers who established their community along Lost Creek. They quickly built their homes from the cottonwoods that grew in the local river bottoms and named the new settlement after a couple of brothers, Patrick and William Jack, who were both veterans of the Texas Revolution, and it was now the county seat. But the town had hardly survived the intervening years, what with the constant Indian raids (especially during the war with all the local troops off fighting elsewhere). It was only now, with the establishment of nearby Fort Richardson that very November, that the locals could finally start living without constant fear for their safety. From the Indians, that is; but life in that place was hardly a rose garden. It was much like "Across the River" at Concho, only bigger—and meaner.

The station keeper pointed me to a nearby boarding house that he promised was "halfway" respectable, and this is where I planned to stay until I could locate the whereabouts of Frank.

"Halfway respectable" proved a stretch indeed, as upon arrival, I found no respectable half present. While I was hoping the "boarding house" would be a cozy and welcoming place along the lines of Mrs. Adams' house in San Antonio, this one was more of what they called back then a "disorderly house"—a place of ill-repute, where the presence of a single lady was more than suspect and her motives quite easily mistook. But I was short of options (and money) and resolved to "hold the fort," as it were, as long as need be.

As luck would have it, the first saloon I happened upon was called "The Little Shamrock," fittingly run by an enterprising young Irishman named John Shanssey. He was a stocky fellow with reddish hair rather like mine in hue. Shanssey was only around twenty-one then, though I later learned that he had certainly gotten around: He was a sometime boxer and had once in Wyoming even fought the famous pugilist known as "Professor" Mike Donovan, in a match refereed by none other than Mr. Wyatt Earp himself. Now here he was running a saloon—amongst other things—on the Texas frontier. And the first glance he gave me upon my appearance in the saloon was not like that of Mr. Veck's at Fort Concho, judging me at once as an aspiring saloon girl; it was rather strangely more like that of recognition. It immediately left me unsettled. Yet once again, following a demonstration of my prowess at cards, I had procured a poker table of my own at "The Little Shamrock" that very evening. With luck, I thought to myself, Frank would walk in at any moment and find me there waiting.

But he did not—neither that night nor the next. So, once again, I bided my time until I thought the occasion ripe to inquire further.

Shanssey spoke with a crisp Irish accent such as I had seldom heard, and like all I later met from that Celtic nation, he was a formidably witty raconteur in want only of an audience (even of one) in order happily to hold court. Listening to him speak, I was hard-pressed to return to work at my table, preferring to sit at the bar and sip Shanssey's Irish whiskey and hear him tell his tales—often relating his adventures as a peripatetic boxer. On one such occasion in the afternoon of the third day, feeling already by now I could trust the young man, I showed him the picture in my locket and related the usual story of my lost cousin, Mike Fogarty. What he then said most nearly knocked me off my seat.

"So you're looking for Frank, are you?"

He chuckled, seeing how taken aback I was. "Worry not, Miss Maud. Or perhaps that should be Miss Carlotta, more like?"

I have seldom ever been caught off my guard and left speechless, but this young man had just "thrown me for a loop." Twice! Before I could think up how to reply, he continued:

"Fear not, your secret's safe here! You see, Frank and I have an understanding. He's working for me now."

I was still reeling with shock by this sudden revelation, but something about Shanssey gave off a good aura, and I felt a sense of relief at someone else being in on my secret. Yet I resolved to stay wary all the same until I felt reassured his motives were sound.

I simply replied, "I'm listening."

"Frank came here from Concho a little while back. He'd heard about the new fort and all the soldiers newly garrisoned here, happily gambling away their weekly salaries. Quite a commotion he made too, Frank did—or "Mike Fogarty" rather, as he was indeed known when we met. So I offered him a poker table here at the Shamrock, and he proceeded to rake in the chips like nobody's business."

Shanssey paused to grab the whiskey bottle and refill our glasses, and seeing he was inclined to continue his story, I resisted the thousand questions boiling up at once. He lifted his glass in toast, and I followed suit.

"Sláinte," he said, and after knocking back the whiskey, he continued: "Frank stood here many a time just where you are now, drinking whiskey and telling tales of his adventures, including the war. Then one night late, when we were having a little lock-in with just the two of us, he opened up and gave me all the goods about himself—including his real name and all about San Antonio and the University Club. And, finally, about a certain lovely red-haired lass called Carlotta."

He gave me such a winsome smile that I knew for sure he was sincere. And that I could trust him and his story.

"A crackin' fine fellow, that Frank," he added. "Makes me laugh till I'm fit to bust." Now he regarded me expectantly, and I finally asked the most obvious question, the one I had been holding back like an Ace of

Spades till the crucial moment.

"Where is Frank now?"

"Off at the Flat."

"I beg your pardon, the flat what?"

"The Flat, over at Camp Wilson. Now being renamed Fort Griffin in honor of the late General Charles Griffin."

"And where is that, Mr. Shanssey?"

I suddenly recalled my whiskey drummer travel companions from the stagecoach trip north from Austin, and their intent to visit Camp Wilson.

"On the Brazos River?"

"Indeed. Along the Clear Fork of the Brazos to be precise, up atop Government Hill. And 'the Flat' down by Collins Creek below the fort is what they call the community nearby—if you can call it that. More like hell on earth, if you ask me. Some even call it 'Sodom of the West.' That town puts Deadwood and Dodge City both to shame when it comes to moral turpitude. But what better place than Hell itself to open a new saloon? Especially when it's right along the cattle trail that runs through there!"

"Why on earth then is Frank there?"

"Ah! As I told you before, he's working for me now. I sent him out to the Flat to help manage my new saloon till I can get there myself." He gave me a sidelong glance. "I regret to say Frank's departure was rather hastened after getting into a nasty fight over a card game here. After that, he had a bullseye on his back. I had no choice but to send him packing—for his own good!"

I rolled my eyes. Typical Frank! Yet Shanssey had hardly uttered those last words before my mind was made up.

"Then that is where I'm going on the first stage west."

Shanssey shook his head adamantly from side to side. "The Brazos is no place for a lass like you to be travelin' to alone. Take it from me."

"I can take care of myself," said I. "Just tell me the name of the saloon where I can find Frank."

Shanssey appeared doubtful, then gave a resigned smirk.

"Well, you have made it this far on your own, I'll give you that. You will find Frank tending bar at the Bee Hive Saloon—right in the midst of town."

"How far is it to Fort Griffin?"

"It is a good sixty miles southwest of here as the crow flies. The next stage leaves in that direction tomorrow morning, if you must."

"Yes, I must!"

"Then please do take extraordinary care, and don't dally along the way. These are perilous parts indeed, especially along the Brazos."

Shanssey poured another whiskey for us both without another word. Then he said, "You will be there within a few days if you're lucky, and the river ain't flooded. Might even get there in time to celebrate the New Year."

"Then I had best be off packing then!"

I started to leave, but Shanssey quickly poured another whiskey for us both.

"First, now get along and make yourself some good money for the road. I'm expecting a big crowd, and all your winnings tonight are yours to keep!"

That inspired me to "play my cards right," indeed, and my winnings that evening were among my best in years. So impressive were the piles of chips I had raked in before quitting time, that a chance remark by a Mexican gambler inspired the name by which (for better or worse) I am remembered to this day. Gazing thoughtfully at my table, he said: "Señorita, with winnings like them, you outta call yourself lotta dinero!

I could not get to sleep that evening, what with the torrent of thoughts about a thousand things at once. What had Shanssey said? Might even get there in time to celebrate the New Year. I could only hope so, especially if it could be with Frank. I had already spent both Thanksgiving and Christmas alone in the middle of nowhere without any friends and was resolved not to bring in the New Year likewise alone.

But later that night, I had an epiphany about a new handle for myself. Mulling over the sound of "lotta dinero" as I lay in bed anxious about the next day's journey, I muttered a string of words to myself: "Lotta ... Lotta Dinero ... Lottie Dinero ... Lottie ..."

Suddenly it came to me as I spoke the words aloud: "Lottie Deno!"

16

THE NEXT MORNING, I looked out from the stagecoach to see on the horizon a strata of colored clouds in a long bar of maroon-tinted glory heralding the sunrise. It was a crisp winter morning, and the ground glinted with silvery frost. As we crossed the bridge over Lost Creek to join the old southwest mail route, I once again felt the exhilarating rush of excited trepidation at the thought of yet a new adventure. An adventure that promised the possibility finally of finding my destiny: one that I could only still hope meant a chance at the kind of love and even happiness that are always so elusive for anyone to find, especially for a young woman. But mostly, I just longed at that moment for some small sense of security—and place— after so long traveling alone.

My traveling companions this time included a small family of rag-tag immigrants speaking in a language that I did not recognize, and who likewise did not appear to speak a word of English. They wore funny large fur hats like I had never before seen. I later learned from the driver during a rest stop that they had come all the way from Russia and were trying to get to California, which they believed was a "Land of Gold"—where if you could only just get there, all of your dreams would come true. Someone had given him a note in Fort Worth to that effect and paid the fare for their passage as far as he could take them.

He said: "I can fetch them far as El Paso, but after that, they're on their own." He shook his head doubtfully. "I can't see how they was hoping to get nowhere else anyway, seeing as how they don't speak no goddam word of American." Then, looking at me thoughtfully, he added: "Mayhap you can learn 'em to speak along the way?"

"I shall try," I said, musing to myself how the good driver could use some "learning" himself. But while I felt little hope at such an endeavor, it seemed all the same a challenge that might at least occupy my time during the journey to Fort Griffin. And so the rest of that day and the next, I found myself in the role of a schoolmarm trying to teach English in a stagecoach full of what turned out to be eager learners; and, sure enough, before too long I had taught them such basic things as how to introduce themselves and how to ask directions to California. My success made me consider the prospect of maybe being a proper teacher someday, if the chance of doing so should ever present itself.

The mesquite-dotted landscape through the North Central Plains was mostly flat, though the "road" was often no more than just a beaten cattle trail and provided for a quite bumpy ride. As we approached the Brazos River, distant storm clouds threatened a rainstorm that I knew would make the river impassable for God knew how long, and at our last stop before reaching the ford, the driver watched the sky anxiously before hastily downing his coffee—which he had poured first into his saucer and swished around to cool off for quick drinking. (An old wartime trick, he said.)

The driver, a rough-hewn but friendly old U.S. Army veteran called Dick Wheeler, pointed at the distant line of clouds. "Them are snow clouds, cold front's a-comin' in directly."

Back in the coach, I and my fellow Russian passengers looked at one another with alarm at the sound of distant rumbling thunder, when we felt a sudden jolt of speed as the driver cracked his whip and exhorted the four-horse team with a stream of expletives. We were all greatly relieved later when the thunder receded into the distance, and upon reaching the ford—in this case, a rock causeway—we found the water low enough for safe crossing.

Finally, in late afternoon of the third day, we trotted down the dusty main avenue into the town they called "the Flat," sprawled out below the new fort on a hill above the Clear Fork of the Brazos. Mr. Wheeler had earlier offered me the chance to sit between him and the lookout upon the driver's seat itself for a better view as we arrived; this created an unintended spectacle for the locals, and by the time I stepped down from the coach I immediately felt disconcertingly out of place with my fine dress and hat and sophisticated demeanor. It seemed like all surrounding eyes were focused upon me, men and womenfolk alike, as I attempted nonchalantly to pretend as if I were aware only of the driver helping me with my clothes trunk.

I waved farewell to my new Russian friends, pleased to hear the chorus of "goodbye, Miss Lottie" in their lovely Slavic intonations as the stagecoach wheeled them away to what I could only pray would be good fortune and happiness.

Nobody offered to help me with the trunk. I thus struggled in a huff to lift it with both arms and turned to seek the inn near the coach stop where Shanssey had promised I need only mention his name to receive "royal" treatment. I soon spotted "O'Connelly's Inn" and found myself once again in a dimly lit vestibule saturated with the putrid smell of untreated buffalo hides stacked in every corner. In fact, the stench of it was everywhere in the Flat, even worse than "Across the River" at Concho. I set down the trunk and felt a sense of déjà vu to find the old innkeeper leering at me with sufficient concupiscence to make even Mr. Veck blush. He spoke with an Irish accent, though it was more rough-edged and unpolished than the lilting music I associated with that of Shanssey.

"Good day to you, miss! Michael O'Connelly, at your service. And what may I be a doing for you?" Before I could reply, I noticed his gaze had dropped a degree south from actual eye contact, so that I quickly crossed my arms to cover my bosom until his eyes met mine again.

"I need decent lodging for tonight at least, and maybe longer. John Shanssey from Jacksboro said if I gave you his name, you would oblige me."

"Young Shanssey sent you to me, did he? Well, good on him! Might have known you were in with that dandy bastard. I shall owe him a pint or two indeed." He chuckled to himself. "And what brings you to a cesspool of a place like this, if you don't mind my asking?"

"I do mind, mister, and there's no need to be snide. Shanssey said you would help, and if you are not inclined to do so, I shall go elsewhere."

"Whoa there, my love! A feisty little lassie at that, I see. Don't mistake me now. I meant no harm by it, miss..."

"Lottie."

"Very well, then, Miss Lottie. I've a nice room upstairs for two bits a night, including breakfast. But seeing as how Shanssey sent ye, I'll throw in some supper as well. The missus is makin' a pot of nice stew even as we speak. You could almost smell it if it weren't for these stinkin' new hides they just brought in this morning." He gestured to the back wall, where at least ten rows of hides were stacked almost to the ceiling. "Serves me right for lodging hide hunters under my roof! But what's a poor feller to do in such a hellhole?"

Trying to ignore his one-sided ramblings, I counted out eight shiny new three-cent nickels and one penny from my purse and stacked them on the counter like miniature poker chips. All I could think of now was my desire to freshen up and finally—at long last—locate Frank.

"There's a wash tub in the room," continued the innkeeper, "and I'll send my two lads up with hot water when you're ready for a bath. Or I might even bring it to you myself!" He gave me a lascivious grin and laughed with a whistle through the wide gap in his teeth.

"Just your lads will be fine," said I, "in one hour, please. Also, may I ask if we are, by chance, anywhere near to The Bee Hive saloon?"

His eyes lit up. "So it's the Hive you're after, eh? Don't that figure now, for such a sweet honey-lass as yourself. Yes indeed, it is just down the road a piece thataways." He gestured to his left. "Right across the road from the Cattle Exchange Saloon, yet another of Shanssey's fine local establishments."

The room was small, dingy, and cold, though from the sole window it did offer a clear view of the street below in either direction. For such a small settlement it was a hive of activity all right. There was a steady beat of hooves over the dirt, some of them teams of horses or mules or even oxen pulling buggies and wagons with their large, many-spoked and creaking wheels. And there was also a steady stream of cattle, including longhorn steers. Squealing hogs ran freely along the road, rooting and grunting and wallowing in the mud. The stench of manure brought up from the street below on the cold breeze was almost intolerable, though actually preferable to that of the piles of untreated buffalo hides almost everywhere one looked. I mused how similar the herd of human and animal traffic appeared (and smelled)—one interconnected stream of living, breathing flesh all seeking, for the most part, one and the same goal: namely food, shelter, and any opportunity to mate—the primary difference for humans being a concomitant lust for gold.

For the human population of this sordid place, the latter two goals were clearly met for many at an establishment I could see just across the street, where an ornate sign over the entrance read "Queen Mab's Place." Its tempting wares stood unashamedly on display upon the front porch in the form of white gowns pulled up despite the cold to reveal fleshy thighs beneath buxom torsos. One of them, a young woman with long dark curly locks and a distinctive-looking face with a prominent nose, happened for some reason to glance upwards and make eye contact with me. I glanced away and quickly drew the curtains, suddenly reminded how hard-pressed I would be in that place not to be taken as usual for a soiled dove myself. All the more reason to locate Frank as soon as possible with the hope of finally regaining at least a modicum of both security and respectability.

A knock on the door put an end to my reverie, and I was pleased to see upon opening it not Mr. O'Connelly but two young sandy-haired and freckled boys who appeared to be twins. They looked to be no more than about ten but had managed to lug upstairs two large pails of hot water, which they now brought into my room and set carefully without any sloshing beside the large wooden tub sitting in the corner by the bed. I thanked them graciously, along with a generous gratuity, and as soon as they were gone gleefully shed my clothes despite the cold and poured myself a much-anticipated bath. I felt like I had all the dust of the Texas plains clinging to my body. The rare luxury of soaking in hot water for a spell felt like a true ablution indeed.

About a half hour of daylight remained as I laced my corset in front of a small mirror. After dressing, I splashed on a few remaining drops of the fine French perfume I had preserved from New Orleans and proceeded downstairs past a gloating Mr. O'Connelly and into the bustling, fetid street. As Mr. Wheeler had predicted, the cold front had arrived, and snow flurries now floated in the air. As I turned left in search of The Bee Hive, several men stopped in their tracks as I waltzed by, whistling and uttering lewd comments. I was appalled by the evident paucity of decent human civility in the Flat. Ignoring them, I stepped up my pace.

Most every storefront or other entrance on both sides of the street had in front of it a line of horses tied up on a hitching rail. Many also displayed gaudy New Year's bunting in anticipation of that night's festivities. It was not far before I approached the Cattle Exchange Saloon on my left, which announced itself even before I saw the sign with a sudden and violent expulsion through its swing-door entrance of two men straightway into the street—where they came just inches from a good trampling by an ox train at that moment passing through, whose driver managed to rein in the beasts just in time. The two men seemed oblivious to all but each other, still locked in the other's arms as they rolled in the snowy dirt and manure, equally intent on landing a well-placed fist in the other's face. A crowd of men (along with a few seedy saloon girls) quickly emerged from the saloon and gathered around the two in a circle. Some cheered while others jeered, and a few placed bets.

For my part, I paid little attention to this silly spectacle as I glanced hopefully across the street—where, sure enough, another batwing saloon entrance beckoned beneath a large sign reading The Bee Hive, illustrated with a colorfully painted image of the same. A long line of horses stood tied up on both sides of the entrance. One looked a lot like Frank's beloved chestnut mare, Nell.

I rushed across the street, dodging various livestock and the shouts of buggy drivers and riders on horseback, until I stopped just beyond the awning-covered entrance to read what appeared to be a poem painted in ornate golden letters. It read:

Within this hive we're all alive,
Good whiskey makes us funny!
If you are dry, step in and try
The flavor of our honey.

It was now on the cusp of night, and a warm yellow light poured outside from within the saloon, along with the sound of a lone fiddle screeching out some unrecognizable tune. But the din of voices—both male and female—punctuated with uproarious laughter felt oddly welcoming. So I took a deep breath, pushed the swing doors to, and stepped inside.

PART V

Queen of the Pasteboards

17

My entrance caused the usual stir, with men's eyes drawn toward me like moths to a sudden flame on a dark night. As usual, I ignored them while proceeding straight to the bar in hopes of finding Frank there. I walked past the fiddle player, to whose tune several cowboys danced in drunken oblivion with saloon girls marking their prey—the latter regarding me with wary eyes.

I got to the bar, and there he was, all right! Even with his back to me, I knew Frank from his still one-of-a-kind Stetson hat and jet-black hair streaming down behind it over his shoulders. I stood there and watched in anxious anticipation of his reaction. For all I knew, he may have taken up with one of those young and perilously seductive girls clearly working for the saloon. Maybe he was even shacking up with one of them upstairs. What would I ever do in such a case? Yet here I was, and there he was, and come what may I was about to find out.

But now he was entirely preoccupied with straightening the many varieties of whiskey bottles behind the bar until I could no longer stand it. I propped my right foot upon the brass rail that ran below the bar and, leaning forward as far as I could, lowered my voice a notch and said: "What's a lady have to do to get served a drink around here?"

Frank did not even pause from his busywork and did not turn around. Instead, he just replied in an annoyed sort of huff, "Hold your horses, miss. You'll get served when I'm damn well ready."

I felt a streak of mischief then and suddenly knew just what to say. I cleared my throat and said in my natural voice: "Look here, mister. Impertinence I simply cannot abide!"

There was a loud clink of glass as Frank dropped the bottle he was at that moment gingerly setting down and swung around to see me smiling at him.

"Carlotta!" he exclaimed.

"Lottie," I corrected him, with a wink. "You must be thinking of somebody else! Though you are Mr. Fogarty, I presume?"

"Well, I'll be ..." he murmured, shaking his head and perceiving the game. Our exchange was now attracting the attention of several onlookers near the bar, as Frank tried to collect himself. He nevertheless stood gazing at me for a long moment, clearly at a loss for words. Yet his joy seemed genuine, at which I felt a sense of relief.

I said, "How about that drink, then?"

"But of course, miss ... Lottie, I believe you said?"

"That is correct, sir. Lottie Deno."

"Deno?" Frank gave me a perplexed look before producing two shot glasses, uncorked the bottle, and proceeded to pour. "From Kentucky." He winked.

"Excellent!"

"Well then, Miss Deno, welcome to the Flat. Or Fort Griffin rather, as they're now calling the town as well as the fort up on the hill."

"Why, thank you kindly, mister. I have spent no small effort getting here neither, of that you may be sure."

"Of that, I have no doubt!" He discreetly touched his glass to mine. "Here's to new beginnings. Just in time for New Year's, too!"

"To new beginnings," I said and shot back the whiskey.

The bar began to get busy, and Frank was forced to attend to his customers while I stood quietly sipping my whiskey and trying to remain inconspicuous, an impossible task as I was constantly aware of the many eyes stealing glances at my back. I was, mercifully, left in relative peace, which I figured had mostly to do with the presence of Frank and his inescapable attentions toward me. It seemed no time before the large grandfather clock near the piano struck eleven, and revelers—anticipating a rowdy countdown—plied one another with drinks.

I had earlier moved to a small table in a corner. Anticipation nearly overwhelmed me, as Frank had promised to slip away later when all were preoccupied with the clock for a rendezvous with me outside the saloon. To bide the time, I took careful note of the card games in progress at tables throughout the barroom, smiling to myself in anticipation of the mincemeat I figured I would soon be making of all those unsuspecting victims.

The hour of midnight soon approached, and as I watched the bar for a sign, I saw Frank discreetly nod as he poured a final round of drinks before the countdown. With all eyes glued on the clock, I slipped from my seat and proceeded quickly behind the throng and outside, where I waited out of sight among the horses. One of them gave a snort, and I knew now it was certainly Nell. "Hello, old girl," I murmured, caressing her mane. The snow had by now picked up and dusted the street white, yet I hardly noticed the cold in my excitement.

Soon afterward, a chorus of gruff, drunken voices began counting down in unison from sixty, and at the twenty-three-second point I saw a flicker of light where the doors swung open, and the silhouette of a man with a very distinctive hat appeared. It was Frank. Nell gave another loud snort as Frank looked over to see me blowing him a kiss and hurried toward me as the countdown inside reached five seconds. He took me in his arms and, as the clock chimed twelve—and voices from all directions joined in singing the most slurred rendition of "Old Lang Syme" imaginable—Frank's lips met mine in the most electrifyingly passionate, lingering kiss I had ever dreamt of in my deepest romantic fantasies.

It was the New Year, and it was snowing. I was in the arms of the man I loved. While I was also in about the worst place a woman could be in the country at that time, all seemed suddenly well in the world. I could hardly have felt any happier than I did at that moment.

18

WE STOOD THERE HOLDING EACH OTHER tightly for some time, all but oblivious to the sudden noise everywhere around us as people poured into the street from every entrance like frenzied ants from a disturbed hill. Men were whooping and hollering, firing guns indiscriminately into the air and sometimes at each other. (For a few such revelers, the new year would prove eternal.)

Frank said, "We'd best mosey back inside, then I can close down the Hive and walk you home. I'll head back to behind the bar, and you follow after a count of ten. It's better we stay discreet for now. But watch out for stray bullets!"

I nodded, musing how best to spot a speeding bullet before first feeling it. I watched as Frank rushed back inside the saloon, instinctively ducking at the sound of gunfire. There was a crash of shattering glass as a bullet struck the saloon's front window just as Frank entered. I lost count then but reckoned there was little time to lose in getting off the street, and I scurried back inside as fast as the cumbersome bustle petticoat beneath my skirt would allow.

Most of the saloon had emptied into the street in the initial excitement. But a few men and saloon girls were gathered around the out-of-tune piano, singing as someone banged out an old-timey Victorian parlor song they used to sing at parties on our plantation in Kentucky.

The last link is broken that bound me to thee,

And the words thou hast spoken
has rendered me free;

That bright glance misleading on others may shine,

Those eyes smiled unheeding when
tears burst from mine.

If my love was deemed boldness, that error is o'er,'

I've witnessed thy coldness and prize thee no more;

I have not loved lightly, I'll think on thee yet,

I'll pray for thee nightly, till life's sun has set.

This brought a sudden pang of nostalgia for the home of my childhood, now forever lost. But it quickly passed as my earlier joy returned, and I knew all that mattered was my life here and now. "New beginnings," Frank had said. I could only pray it would prove so.

On Frank's advice, I asked Mr. O'Connelly the next day about more permanent accommodation, and he obliged with an offer of renting "a very fine house" to me at a quite reasonable rate. Intrigued, I walked with him some ways down the main avenue (soon thereafter called "Griffin Avenue") until, to my dismay, we reached a row of decrepit-looking little buildings on the very north edge of town by the river. From the look of the local occupants and the rather seedy characters lurking thereabouts, I could tell right off we were in that particular district endemic to most every town of any size that the advent of electricity would soon illumine in red.

We came to a small wooden shanty that overlooked the Clear Fork of the Brazos at the end of a long row of nearly identical structures. As Mr. O'Connelly opened the door, he seemed taken aback by my deliberate look of incredulity. However, as we entered, I found the place surprisingly cozy. Recalling the sordid hut at Concho, I had expected the worst. But it was a two-room house replete with a comfortable-looking bed (including thick, elegantly woven, and warm-looking quilts) and a shiny new chamber pot—along with a small table and several chairs, a chest of drawers, and shelves with assorted cutlery and crockery and a few tin plates. A kerosene lantern hung from the middle of the ceiling. Most importantly, there was a stone hearth for warmth and a little iron stove for cooking. I quickly resolved that this would do quite well for my immediate purposes, and so without a second thought, I turned and smiled at the relieved Mr. O'Connelly.

"This will do," I said, and by that afternoon, I had returned with my trunk and begun to prepare for yet another fresh start in a strange new place.

I had brought a letter from Shanssey to Frank formally requesting he hire me in my usual role as a house dealer and percentage player at the Bee Hive Saloon, and that very night found me dealing cards at a table in the saloon's upstairs gambling hall. Depending on the whims of any day's particular crowd, when not busy at the Faro box, you could find me playing poker (and sometimes "Seven-Up" and the Mexican game of "Monte") or even spinning a crude roulette wheel Frank had set up.

Despite the habitually rough crowd, I felt safe knowing Frank was behind the bar keeping an eye on everyone. And among the locals, at least, word seemed to get around (though largely unspoken) that I was "Fogarty's girl" and thus not to be messed with. (Word had also gotten around about Frank's short fuse—and his ubiquitous Bowie knife—when it came to miscreant behavior inside the saloon.) I also picked up yet a new local nickname about town: Frank informed me they were now calling me the "Queen of the Pasteboards." (I heard others even called me the "Gambling Queen of Hearts.") Either way, being referred to as the local "Queen" suited me just fine!

The tensest occasions usually occurred on Saturdays, when the boys from the local fort up on nearby Government Hill got paid and came down to play. It did not help that, at that time, they included colored soldiers of the 10th Cavalry Regiment—the so-called "Buffalo Soldiers" I had previously encountered en route to the frontier. Many of the local cowpunchers and other drifters and grifters drawn to the Flat for various (often dubious) motives were erstwhile Confederate veterans. Some among them looked askance at these proud and freewheeling "darkies" as they called them. This and other insulting terms they spoke in cowardly fashion amongst themselves behind the Buffalo soldiers' backs, for fear of being shot. These same former Rebs likewise resented the white Federal soldiers who often stood with their dark-skinned comrades so soon after the "War of Northern Aggression" (as the Rebs called it). When they were deep in their cups, such men were dangerous indeed when tempers flared—especially coupled with a losing hand when the stakes were high. Frank often had to turn them out onto the street where differences were settled by violent fist fights or—all too often—gunfire.

But on one occasion, while Frank was away in Jacksboro on business with Shanssey, I had a close brush with death.

I was dealing Faro one night in the smoky gambling hall of Wilson & Mathews' Saloon (just down the road from the Bee Hive) when a scuffle over the pot turned deadly. The hall was full of spectators—local gamblers, mostly—as the poker game had been announced in advance between two notorious tinhorn gamblers: Texan "Smoky Joe" and the Arizona cardsharp "Monte Bill." They were both quite uncouth in appearance, and I had had a bad feeling all evening that the night was destined for a fight. And so it was.

I was sitting at the table adjacent when things got suddenly ugly between the two men. Everyone at my table put down their cards and turned their attention to the fracas. It seemed that with five hundred dollars in the pot, Monty had dared Smoky to raise the limit, to which Smoky had agreed and bet every last dollar he had. The pot held almost one thousand dollars when Monte—calling his hand—laid down a pair of queens along with three aces. Smoky dropped his own hand and jerked out his gun, one of the new Colt .45 "Peacemaker" revolvers then used by the U.S. military.

"Cheated by a sneakin' coyote from the badlands!" he yelled. "Ringing in a cold deck and marked cards when playing a gentleman!" Then Smoky called to the porter, a young colored boy. "Take the pot for me, John."

But Monte was having none of it. "You can't play that game of bluff on me, you damn Texas bullwhacker!"

At that, he pulled out his own six-shooter, and both guns fired in an instant. The crowded room erupted in panic as people scattered and ran for cover away from the flying bullets. I knocked my chair backward as I pushed away from my table, thinking at first to escape through the entrance along with everybody else. But a new notion crossed my mind, and I cowered down in a corner of the room instead. Just in the nick of time, too, as a bullet ricocheted off the wall where I was standing a moment before.

I crawled under a table and stayed put there until the shooting finally stopped. All that remained of poor Smoky and Monte were two dead bodies sprawled out on the floor in a pool of blood.

As usual in Fort Griffin, the "law" arrived after the shooting had ended.

When the sheriff, a local lawman by the name of Bill Cruger, finally entered, everyone else had fled and the hall was otherwise deserted. He looked perplexed to find me sitting alone and unperturbed back at the Faro table, counting my chips.

"I heard what happened here, Miss Lottie! Why the hell didn't you skedaddle with everyone else?"

"It was too late for me to get out once the shooting started, sheriff. But I was safe from bullets under the table."

"Well," he said, doubtfully, "you do have some kind of nerve, old girl! I don't reckon I would have taken my chances in such a dogfight as that."

"From the looks of it, I don't reckon you would either, sheriff!" I winked at him, and I swear he blushed. "But then," I added, "you have never been a desperate woman."

He picked up the pot and shook it, clearly surprised to find it empty. He eyed me suspiciously for a moment. Then he began to laugh softly to himself.

"That may be," he said, "but you'd best clear out of here now, before the coroner arrives to view these worthless stiffs."

"All right, sheriff, I shall. I suddenly feel quite sleepy!"

As he stooped down to inspect the bodies, I quickly picked up my reticule and hid it from his view as I walked out. It seemed best that the sheriff did not see it, being visibly filled to the brim as it was with greenbacks.

Despite almost getting myself shot, it had been quite a good night!

19

THAT WAS THE FIRST TIME I nearly got shot. The second time I have already described at the opening of this chronicle of my adventures, when Mr. John Henry "Doc" Holliday arrived back in town.

He had already spent some time in Fort Griffin previously and was forced to leave following a skirmish. But such was the nature of "justice" in those frontier days that there was something of an unspoken "statute of limitations"—whereby after sufficient time, any given transgression tended to be forgotten once one's "Wanted" bills became buried under the hundreds of others sure to soon follow. Such was the case with Frank in San Antonio (as we had since learned from his brother Will), and this was the case now with Doc.

Where all he had been off to in the meantime was anyone's guess (some said Colorado), but the one thing for certain is that he now arrived from Jacksboro, from whence—according to Shanssey, who kept himself informed about all the dealings at his saloon there—Doc had likewise departed upon some necessary compulsion.

But there was clearly something else that drew Doc back to Fort Griffin at his earliest opportunity. And that something was the woman known about town as "Big Nose Kate." The truth be told, I felt that moniker to be rather unfair. Shapely is how I would describe her notorious facial appendage: shapely in an attractive Eastern European way (she was of Hungarian stock), along with her voluptuous hair that flowed down her back in dark, curly locks.

After working a spell at "Queen Mab's Place" brothel–often in cahoots with a notoriously violent whore called Scarface Fanny–Kate had long since gained local prominence as a "free-lance" whore. She first met Doc when he was holding court at Shanssey's Saloon during his previous visit, and immediately attached herself to him as a kind of permanent paramour. And while Big Nose Kate was always welcomed with open arms by most of the local saloon proprietors (including Shanssey), I had seen to it that she was strictly forbidden from so much as setting one dainty little foot of hers in the Bee Hive. I admit this had as much to do with my wish to keep her away from Frank as much as for any moral reasons I may have professed. I trusted Frank, I truly did–to the extent, of course, that a woman may ever really trust any man. However, with a woman like Big Nose Kate around, I figured it best not to hedge my bets. (It did not help that she was somewhat younger than I to boot.)

It was for this reason she held a particular animosity towards me–along with the local gossip that I had my sights set on Doc Holliday. In Kate's mind, that was the reason I had banned her originally from the Bee Hive, so that when Doc was still in town, I could have him all to myself there. While he clearly did have a "thing" for me, I simply finessed this to my advantage when it came to enticing him into betting at my table whenever he visited the Bee Hive gambling resort.

I cannot, however, deny that I did find Doc a handsome piece of work, sickly desperado though he was. He was still a young man then (really just a boy), tall and slim and blue-eyed and with hair almost as red as mine.

Doc, bless his heart, had already experienced much travail. Once an aspiring young dentist trained at the finest schools, he was forced to give up his practice when his tuberculosis became impossible to conceal from patients. He headed West in hopes the dryer climate might slow his lungs' deterioration, where he turned a talent for gambling into his sole livelihood. It was in the West that other, more violent talents, quickly became manifest as well.

Now he was back in the Flat, and it was not too long before he moseyed one night into the Bee Hive. To make matters worse, Frank was still out of town, a fact of which Kate was very much aware. She had secretly followed Doc as far as the entrance, and after standing outside a spell nursing her suspicions with copious swigs of whiskey from the small flask she always carried in her purse next to her gun, her jealousy spilt over into rage, and it was soon the gun she reached for next.

I knew it would not be long before Doc decided to play a turn or two of Faro. I watched him from the corner of my eye as he downed a few quick shots of whiskey at the bar. And the moment he set his eyes upon me, I shot him a coquettish smile and batted my eyelids at him (an art I had long ago cultivated). As usual, it worked. Doc beelined his ever so charming derrière straight to my long Faro table.

Everyone watched Doc as he swaggered toward me, and the piano player gave me a sidelong wink from where he sat playing in his corner. The other gamblers sitting at the table watched Doc warily and reluctantly made room for the celebrated–or notorious, depending on whom you asked–Georgia gentleman. His colorful velvet waistcoat and bow tie stood out in pleasant contrast against the other gamblers' dull combination of black and white. And his pale-faced frailty somehow made him all the more alluring, so that I longed just once to reach out and take hold of that dark leonine handlebar mustache and pull him into a kiss. As he hovered a moment over the table, surveying the stacks of chips, he winked at me. "Mind if I join y'all, Miss Lottie?"

I nodded at an empty chair right next to me. Despite my sudden feeling of inner excitement, I feigned a professional air of nonchalance as Doc pulled out the chair and dropped himself into it like it was a horse's saddle, all the while fixing his eyes on mine with a look that liked to melt my heart. He was, as always, winsome, handsome, and drunk. Doc glanced quickly over the layout of green felt with its thirteen squares of painted cards. Then he pulled out a thick wad of bills from the waistcoat pocket hidden beneath his jacket–the same pocket where I knew he always kept his nifty double-barreled .41-calibre derringer–and casually tossed fifty dollars down onto the table. I am afraid I must have eyed his money as lustily as I had Doc himself just moments before, but this time both would have to wait. We had hardly gotten going with the game when we were interrupted by such a disturbance that all eyes in the bar turned toward the entrance. The piano music suddenly stopped, which was never a good omen in any saloon.

I figured there would be trouble just as soon as I heard the unmistakable bark of Big Nose Kate when she burst through the batwing doors shouting Doc's name. The moment she spotted Doc sitting at my table, her eyes saw red—and that red was me: the color of my dress as well as my locks. I knew something about the perilous nature of a woman aflame with jealousy, and I also knew that, like any sensible woman, Kate always packed a pistol hidden somewhere on her person. Mine was hidden in my boot, and I reached for it now as she barreled toward me, wrecking several tables (and their occupants) in her wake. Kate was also well-known as a sure shot with her gun, no matter how liquored up she usually was—and now her long-barreled "Peacemaker" revolver had my name on it.

Everyone quickly fled our table apart from Doc and myself. The rest of the barroom was now so quiet you could hear the crickets outside. As I stared at the barrel of the gun in my face, my right forefinger found the cold steel of the pistol trigger in my boot. Kate glared at me with eyes red as a mad sow, small as they seemed on both sides of that notorious nose. Then she shouted:

"How dare you seek to steal my man's affections, you stinkin' redhead whore!"

Doc nervously fiddled with his pocket watch and coughed into a finely woven silk handkerchief, while I looked calmly down at the cards and flipped one before slowly looking back up at Kate and utterly losing my carefully cultivated aura of civility.

"Why, you low-down, slinkin' slut! If I stepped in a pile of soft cow manure, I wouldn't even clean this boot on that bastard. I'll show you a thing or two!"

Faster than she could blink, I pulled out the pistol from my boot and aimed it right back at her.

Then, with the agility of a wild mountain goat, Doc jumped out of his seat and stepped right between Kate and me and our now almost smoking barrels. A second later and I reckon Doc would be sporting two new bullet holes in that fine sleek hide of his.

Kate now aimed her fury—and her gun—at Doc. She shouted, "Have you no conscience, you perfidious flapdoodle?"

Doc coughed again and smiled. "I coughed out all my conscience long ago."

Kate rolled her eyes and grimaced at him, lowering her gun until it pointed directly below his shiny belt buckle.

"One word more out of you and you'll be speakin' in the soprano, sugar!"

Yet Doc's calm demeanor was sufficient to diffuse her wrath, and he gently pushed our firearms downward until they both pointed at the floor.

"C'mon, darlin'," he gently exhorted, Kate's painful threat notwithstanding. "Why don't you kiss me, Kate, and shoot some fine whiskey instead? Then we can try our luck bucking the tiger at Faro." He glanced at me with a mischievous glint in his eyes. "And then just let the chips fall where they may!"

Kate finally relented and dropped the gun back in her purse before moving over to kiss Doc. I followed suit, depositing my own pistol back in its hiding place in my boot. Just like that, the crowd cautiously returned to their tables, the piano player resumed his playing, and soon it was business as usual. I proceeded to shuffle the cards and load them into the metal dealing box as if nothing had happened, and once the bets were all placed on the layout, the game began.

20

WHEN FRANK RETURNED he was none too pleased to hear about my close call with Kate. But then he went and lost everything we had on a drunken bet with Doc Holliday.

Doc, knowing full well Frank's fondness (weakness might be the better word) for good whiskey, brought in a bottle one afternoon and got Frank—whom Doc still knew under his alias "Mike Fogarty"—good and drunk. Frank was bartending, but the saloon was all but empty, and the two fellow Georgians sat drinking and smoking

(Doc with a cigar and Frank with his pipe) and playing a game of "High Dice" at the bar to while away the time. They were also enjoying the rare luxury of slurping from the half-shell cold oysters that had been brought up from the coast and kept fresh in the town's ice house, filled each winter with ice extracted from the frozen Brazos and insulated underground with packed sawdust.

They had a little conference over their dice, the outcome of which was even more than just Frank's money at stake. Alas, I was not there to stop Frank from making such a rash bet, being upstairs dealing in the gambling hall. I only learned belatedly from Kate (who had listened in on it all) what he had gone and agreed to with Doc.

"Let us up the ante," Doc had added. "I propose playing not only for your money, but your whole outfit to boot. If I win, you are to vamoose the Bee Hive forthwith. Regardless, the winner is to stake his defeated adversary one thousand dollars."

"That seems an agreeable offer," Frank drunkenly replied. "How strong are you, may I ask?"

"Thirty thousand dollars in thirty bills," Doc replied. "And may I inquire how strong are you, sir? I likewise prefer knowing how long a trail I've got to travel."

"My roll is about forty thousand strong."

"That is comforting to hear!" Doc retorted. "If I lose, I still keep an even thousand. Yet if I win, you hit the trail with a thousand, while I'm the new owner of your whole kit and caboodle!"

"So be it!"

The two men shook hands on it and agreed to commence their game that evening.

Needless to relate, I was, of course, furious with Frank when I heard the news. He had sobered up sufficiently by now to have grave misgivings about the bet he had made with Doc.

"You did what?" I exclaimed.

"I'm sorry, sugar. I don't know what got into me."

I picked up the now empty whiskey bottle from the bar. "I do! Now look here, Frank, you must end this."

He looked at me apologetically. "Can't now, we already shook on it. Win or lose, the game is on!"

I pouted for a moment but suddenly lit upon an idea. I quickly pulled Frank aside.

"If he breaks you, he has to go on and break me too. I have a bundle of three thousand bucks I've saved up, and he's got to get it all before the game is closed. Tell Doc that!"

Frank appeared horrified at the thought. He shook his head and said, "That would be downright dishonorable of me, to have to bring in a woman to save my ass! No, I made this bet, and it's now my cross to bear."

He turned to walk away, but I held him by the sleeve and pleaded with him as my eyes teared up. (Another art I had cultivated that I knew gentlemen could not resist.)

"I have no doubt you'll win on your own, like you always do," said I, appealing to Frank's not-insignificant ego. "But please do this for me Frank, if only so I can feel a part of it too!" I smiled and blinked at him hopefully through my tears.

Frank hesitated a moment and, as usual, capitulated. "Well, all right, dammit," he said. Then he winked. "But you'll owe me one, darlin'!" I winked back and smiled, then watched anxiously as he paced over to Doc.

"There's a bet I overlooked, Doc." Frank nodded toward me. "My partner yonder. It's only a matter of three thousand, but if things fall out that I wind up down and out, you will have to break Miss Lottie before the saloon's all yours."

Doc looked doubtful as Kate shook her head no at him. She said, "Don't you dare do it, Doc!"

To my surprise and relief, Doc's face broke into a wide grin. "That is eminently satisfactory!" he returned. "And I freely add that your little partner is a dead game sport to take so small a fortune and—win all or lose all—go after more than twenty times as much. Quite the little optimist, that Miss Lottie."

"That she is!" concurred Frank, suddenly absorbed in a close scrutiny of the floor as I glared at him.

A full house soon awaited upstairs where a large crowd gathered in the gambling hall. Word had gone quickly round Fort Griffin (both the town and the garrison itself) that Doc Holliday was out for Mike Fogarty's entire game, betting all he had against the Bee Hive saloon and all Fogarty's money at once. As I heard one onlooker comment:

"They'll set a limit higher than a cat's back, I warrant you."

Commented another, "It is a duel to the death, all right!"

The crowd immediately shushed as we all reached my accustomed table, Doc and Frank together followed by me and Kate. Once Frank had taken his place at the layout, the game began. For my part, as I usually did whenever Frank was dealing, I took my place on the stool behind him as his lookout (just like Mary had always done for me long before). Kate stood behind Doc, whispering some sweet nothing or other in his ear and kissing his neck. She had had a tipple or two already. But Doc by this time was focused on the game at hand and impatiently shook her off.

"Make yourself useful and fetch me a hot toddy!" he ordered. Kate gave an angry huff but reluctantly complied. Doc now turned his attention to Frank.

"What limit do you give me?"

Doc coughed, then continued. "Be liberal. I ain't more than a year to live anyhow, so I've got to play high and hard. If I were in robust health now with a long and useful life before me, why then the usual figures would do. Considering my wasted health, however, I sure hope you'll say something like the even thousand."

"I'll do better than that!" returned Frank, slapping the deck of cards in the Faro box. "I'll let you fix the limit to suit yourself. Make it the ceiling if the spirit so moves you."

"That is mighty generous! And to mark my appreciation thereof, I'll just naturally take every risk of splits and put ten thousand in the pot, coppered, and ten thousand in the big square, and ten thousand, also coppered, on the high card."

Everyone watching drew a deep breath at once as Doc laid out the money. Thirty thousand in three ten-thousand-dollar bets, all on the layout at once in stacks of crisp new thousand-dollar bills! Then he placed two copper coins on the "coppered" bets so that if he chose the "correct" losing card, he would be paid 1-to-1. (The same went for betting on the "high card.")

That amount was hitherto a record at the Bee Hive so far as I knew. But there it all lay on the table, where both Doc and Frank now sat scrutinizing each other's emotionless faces.

"Turn your game!" said Doc, leaning back to light a cigar.

Frank made the turn. The top card on the deck in the box was a ten-spot. This was the "soda card," the top card that was discarded to show the next card in the deck (which was the "losing" card, and any bets placed on it were lost to the dealer). The next cards fell "seven-king" and Doc proceeded to win all along, so just like that Frank was out thirty thousand after showing only three cards.

Kate had become all the more amorous (and drunk) as the game proceeded. "That's my boy!" she said, kissing Doc again.

"Easy as pullin' teeth!" he mused.

I looked at Frank. His face was calm as a statue, being as usual too finely fibered a sport to allow so much as an eyelash to quiver. Doc was equally unemotional, as Frank shoved over three yellow chips.

Frank said, "Call 'em ten thousand each." Then he

waited for Doc to place his next bets.

"Since you have exactly that sum left in your treasury," observed Doc, "I reckon I'll let one of these yellow tokens go, coppered, on the high card again. You double or break right here."

I could barely contain my anxiety, holding my breath until Frank won the turn and took in that ten-thousand-dollar chip.

"Seeing I'm still playing on velvet," said Doc languidly, as if only half interested, "I'll go twenty thousand on the high card, open. This time I'll omit the copper."

The first card to show was a deuce. It was now ten to one that Frank would win. But when the next card showed an ace the watching crowd gasped, and Frank nearly fell from his chair. The bank was broke, and to signify as much Frank turned his box on its side, counted out forty thousand dollars to Doc, and got up from the dealer's chair. By this point Kate was ecstatic, hugging Doc around the neck and kissing him again. This time he reciprocated, all the while grinning at Frank.

Doc said, "You look about as happy as a bulldog chewing on a wasp."

And that is when I sprang into action. I slid off my lookout's stool and into Frank's now vacant chair at the table. I turned the Faro dealing box back upright, took out the deck of cards, shuffled it and loaded it back into the dealing box—open at the top so all could see the first card's face in the deck. I looked up at Doc and gazed as deeply as I could into his steely blue eyes.

I said, "And now you've got to break me. Also, we restore the status quo and the limit retreats to an even hundred dollars."

Doc took off his hat and tossed away his cigar. "Are you really as lucky as Fogarty says you are, Miss Lottie?" He chuckled, then coughed again.

"I am."

"Then I feel honored to find myself across the layout from so much spirit and beauty. A limit of one hundred dollars, you say, and your word is law! As a first step, give me three thousand dollars' worth of chips and make em' fifty dollars each. I'll take the same chance on splits as I did with Fogarty, and I want a hundred on every card, middle to win against the ends."

I nodded and began to deal, winning from the jump. I took in three bets to lose one to the turn. Doc then called the turn for the limit and lost. The cards went into the box again and the next deal ensued. So it continued, and I coppered every bet, beating Doc hard for half an hour. Once I saw I was in luck, I decided to press it some.

I said, "The limit's five hundred! Come after me, Doc?"

Doc gave a slight bow toward me like he had just accepted a compliment. "I'm after you, darlin', and here I come a-running!" Down went his money all over the layout, only now it was five hundred instead of one.

Doc smiled. "Allow me to buy you a whiskey, sweetheart."

"I never touch the stuff," I lied, "thank you all the same." A whiskey is what I needed more than anything else right then, but I had to keep the public reputation

I had so carefully forged. I also must needs stay fully sober and clear-headed. "Thank you all the same!"

At the end of another hour, Doc was still losing. I sized up my roll, and it was a little over forty thousand strong, right where Frank had stood at the start of his game earlier. I paused a moment just before putting the deck back in the box for another deal. I looked thoughtfully at Doc, considering my options.

This all proved too much for Frank, who had appeared on the brink of fits ever since the play began. He leaned over and whispered into my ear emotionally.

"Don't raise the limit, Lottie! That's where I was weak from the start, I ought never to have thrown away the limit."

I smiled at Frank and nodded. "Just trust me," I said. He stepped back, looking worried. He was, however, in for a shock when I next spoke to Doc.

"Go as far as you like, Doc. The bridle's off the horse!"

Frank was in near hysterics. "Lottie, no!"

I gestured to him to settle down. Doc just gave another one of his polite little bows over the table.

"Much obliged to you, Miss Lottie!" he said. "I'll make you the same three bets I made to Mr. Fogarty there. Ten thousand, coppered, in the pot. Ten thousand, open, in the big square. And ten thousand on the high card, likewise coppered."

I felt so nervous I found myself struggling to catch my breath when I next spoke. "And now, as then," I said, pointing to the top card, "the ten-spots' the soda card." Despite my effort to hide it, my right hand was shaking as I carefully reached to lift up the top card. But my luck held: The cards fell "king-seven."

One of the observers gathered around the table suddenly shouted for all to hear: "The bank wins!" And with that the whole hall erupted in a chorus of applause and cheers.

I looked back up at Frank. "There, hon," I said, along with a deep sigh of content. "There is your bank again, only it's thirty thousand stronger than it was when you started! Did I not say to trust me?"

"Your bank, ladybird," Frank replied.

"Well, our bank then! What's the difference? Did you not say we were partners?" I motioned to the bar and gave a gleeful shout. "Drinks on the house!" The hall burst into cheers again as everyone rushed to the bar.

I glanced back at Doc, now looking dejected, with a glum Kate by his side. He was cleaned out.

"Cheer up, Doc," said I, "And enjoy the free drinks while you may."

"After all," rejoined Frank, "you've bankrolled the house tonight!"

Doc just smirked and took a sip of his toddy. He acted like a retort was forthcoming, but then he fell into a fit of coughing.

Frank said, "That cough sounds like the prelude to a funeral."

Doc got up without another word and quickly departed, along with an anxious-looking Kate following in his trail.

But Doc Holliday was not one to let bad luck keep him down long. The next day he got into a poker game with an army officer stationed at the fort and won five hundred dollars and a diamond ring.

Not long afterward, however, Doc and Kate were obliged to make their precipitous exit from Fort Griffin. Doc got into a fight with a man named Ed Bailey after detecting the latter cheating at poker. When Bailey pulled his gun, Doc jerked out a knife and—as Wyatt Earp would later famously write—"with one sideways sweep had caught Bailey just below the brisket." (I am afraid to say Doc had learnt that little knife trick from Frank.)

It mattered not that Doc was clearly in the right, having acted in self-defense. Bailey's death provoked his local friends to form a lynch mob and seek vigilante justice, and it was only with the help of Big Nose Kate that he managed to escape. Kate distracted both the mob and the lawmen holding Doc by setting a nearby barn ablaze. Wielding her six-shooter, she rescued Doc and they fled the four hundred miles to Dodge City, where Doc knew his friend Wyatt Earp was serving as assistant marshal.

I later heard Doc's attempt at reviving his dental practice in Dodge was an unqualified disaster.

21

ONE NIGHT SOON AFTERWARD, while dealing cards at my table, I felt the strange sensation of being closely watched. I looked across the gambling hall to see a pair of icy cold eyes staring at me with a look that sent an ominous chill through my bones. Cold eye rather: One of the eyes was clouded over with an eerily white hue, adding to the frightful menace of his gaze. They belonged to a sinister-looking man whose scruffy appearance indicated he had just returned after weeks in the wilderness. Around his hat was a rattlesnake skin—complete with head and rattle—wrapped as a band. And from the long buffalo wool chaps he wore, I assumed he must be a hide hunter.

Observing this exchange of looks, one of the gamblers at my table (an old buffalo hunter himself), warned: "Best steer clear of that fellow, miss. That's one of them Comanchero bandits from out yonder over the Clear Fork in the *Llano Estacado* badlands."

He gestured vaguely in a random direction behind us.

"I hear tell him and his men come into town late last night after terrorizing a small camp of settlers who were passing through. They was drunk and a-hollerin' and shootin' everyone they could find, the women and young'uns too. They'll kill you as soon as look at you, or worse even. You beware of them boys, mark my words." Then, seeing my alarm, he added: "They ain't staying long though, not with a fort full of soldiers nearby watching out for the likes of them murderin' thieves!"

I glanced back across the room, but the evil-eyed Comanchero was gone.

Yet for the most part—and despite the perennial danger, to which I had become accustomed ever since arriving in Texas—I enjoyed having a daily routine in one place again, especially now that it included Frank. He would slip out of the saloon each evening after closing time and make his way in the darkness to my little shack, which might as well have been a luxurious palace as far as I was concerned when I was in his arms all through the night. Then early each morning, as the "Reveille" bugle wake-up call sounded from the fort upon the hill, I would make strong coffee for him before he left at dawn to prepare the Bee Hive for a new day.

To my surprise, I even made a new friend of a former acquaintance whom I one day encountered while shopping for a pair of new boots at Glesk Boot Shop, an inviting and leather-infused boutique next to the dry goods and saddlery store operated by the local sutler (who also had a store up on the hill serving the fort).

The weather had warmed up some and melted the snow, though the streets and especially the main avenue remained terribly muddy. Shopping for boots there also that day was Emily, the doctor's wife I recalled from the stagecoach to Concho. Her husband was now posted at Fort Griffin.

She suggested we meet for tea at the nearby Occidental Hotel, the closest thing to civilization that side of the Brazos, and a popular place for the officer's wives to meet for bridge and to share gossip about the local goings on. I was soon invited to join them, and it was all I could do to allow the other ladies occasionally to win at bridge!

This soon became a weekly routine, for which I felt quite grateful as Emily's friendship and acceptance of me—an otherwise lowly "lady gambler" from town—gave me an aura of rare respectability among the women of the Flat. (The locals all knew full well that such a lady as Emily would never be seen to associate with a *nymphe du pavé!*)

In my newfound happiness, I had almost forgotten my anxiety over Johnny. But he had not forgotten about me, as I would soon discover. It was in early February, not long after the old Camp Wilson was officially rechristened "Fort Griffin" on the sixth of that month with military fanfare and gun salutes, that I first heard news of Johnny's arrival—though in a far different fashion than I could ever have expected.

22

HERE ON THE EDGE of the frontier, the "marshal" was merely a local figure elected by civilians—hardly an official United States Marshal such as those found in larger towns like Dodge City—and the later Shackelford County was not yet formed. (Despite the nearby fort, the military avoided local affairs for the most part, being preoccupied themselves with their official directive to fight Indians and bandits for the protection of settlers and livestock.) The marshal therefore had little real authority beyond enforcing (if he wished to stay both elected and alive) the will of the mob—soon thereafter itself organized more formally into a notorious "Vigilance Committee." The so-called "peace officers" were often no more than ne'er-do-wells themselves, using their position to further their own nefarious self-interests as horse thieves and cattle rustlers. The only system of frontier "law" at that time was therefore usually meted out as vigilante justice—where the simple pointing of a finger served as judge, jury and executioner all at once, leaving the accused to plead his case from the wrong end of a rope.

But it was the marshal who was expected to rein in the outlaws and troublemakers who threatened what little civility existed in such parts, and I was shocked when he brought into the Bee Hive one day a satchel of "Wanted" notices bearing the photograph of Johnny Golden! I had asked Shanssey to send word immediately if Johnny turned up in Jacksboro, but there were no telegraph lines connecting the frontier forts yet and mail deliveries were few and far between. He was thus unlooked for, and I was caught completely off guard.

I could only stare at the poster in disbelief as Marshal Bill Gilson nailed it to the noticeboard by the entrance. Frank walked up at that moment from behind and, after a quick glance at the poster over my shoulder, asked perfunctorily: "What's he wanted for, Marshal?"

"Murder," replied the marshal, stepping back to survey his handiwork. "Also a known horse thief. Kilt a card sharp with his knife out in Waco, over a game of poker. Word has it he's headed this way now. Searchin' for a woman, they say. Keep an eye out, will you?" Frank nodded, and with a cursory tip of his hat the marshal hurried out with the posters to continue his rounds.

I was so distracted pondering the "Wanted" notice that I did not even hear Frank speaking to me.

"Lottie? I said how about a quick drink before getting back to work?"

I turned around, startled. "What? No, I ... I am feeling quite suddenly not at all well." He looked a combination of concerned and baffled as I turned away and rushed out of the saloon, not glancing back as I paced down the avenue in no particular direction. I did not know what Johnny planned to do once he found me. Yet one thing was certain. My past had finally caught up with me and there was no place left to hide.

Despite all the time that had passed since last seeing him, I found it hard to imagine Johnny as a murderer. But there it was: His face was now all over town declaring him wanted dead or alive for murder. Over something as meaningless as a poker dispute. I recalled, however, the way he had so suddenly changed after returning from his first real fighting in the war, and the pain in his eyes that had then disturbed me so.

Of course, I had seen it in Frank too that day he killed a man right in front of me with his knife. Even though that was clearly both in self-defense and in protection of me, I did find the apparent facility of his actions somewhat frightening. I had since wondered if the horrors he himself saw in the trenches of war had not rendered violence for him a thing of less consequence than it is for those innocent of such experience. I bitterly realized that the only two men I had ever loved both eventually wound up on a "Wanted" poster, and now I was destined to be caught in the crossfire when they met. I wished now, too, that I had just been upfront with Frank about Johnny back in San Antonio when I had had the chance. "The truth will out," as the Bard wrote, no matter how hard you try to hide it while hoping otherwise—and making it so much the worse when it finally does.

I felt a piercing sense of dread upon returning to the Bee Hive in time for my appointment at the Faro table and had just begun dealing cards when there was a commotion downstairs. I heard Johnny's voice before I saw him.

"Where is she?" I heard him shout. His voice sounded frantic, desperate even. I wondered again—and still do—why he was so keen to find me after so much time had passed, or why he could not simply accept that I was no longer waiting for him and that he should just move on with his life. But everything then happened so quickly that I still shake my head in disbelief upon recollection of that day.

I heard the heavy thud of boots and the chime-like clink of spurs on the wooden steps getting louder as they stomped upwards to the gambling hall. Then I saw him. The first thing I noticed as his head appeared at the top of the stairs was the wildness in his eyes, accentuated by the torn front rim of his dusty dark hat. He had a scraggly beard (without mustache), already graying at the edges despite his years, and there was a deep scar on his right cheek just below the eye. He was also somewhat taller now than the short former jockey I remembered.

Johnny quickly surveyed the tables of the gambling hall until he spotted me, and the moment his eyes met mine he strode across the room toward me. When Frank appeared on the staircase landing in pursuit, the other patrons at my table jumped to their feet and backed away.

Frank shouted: "Get the fuck out of my saloon, you sonuvabitch!"

I hoped for a moment that Frank might stop Johnny and take him away before he had the chance to say anything to me. But to my dismay, once it was clear that it was in fact I who was the object of Johnny's search, Frank just stopped in his tracks to see and to hear what followed. "Go fetch the marshal," he said to someone standing behind him.

Johnny gave me a long stare in apparent disbelief, before his thin lips gave way to a grin.

"Why, hello Carlotta! Or shall I call you Maud? Or is it Lottie now? I can't keep track. And what the hell is a lady like you doing in a sleazy doggery such as this, anyway?"

"Johnny, I thought you were ..." I was at an unwonted loss of words and found myself stuttering. I knew I was caught and there was nothing else now for it. Johnny just laughed, and I froze with a feeling both of embarrassment and shame to have Frank hear what he said next.

"Dead? I might as well be," mused Johnny. "You've given me quite a chase since our last night in Detroit. And whatever happened to your promise to wait for me in San Antonio?"

In a flash I determined to tell him then and there—and for all to hear—the story of my life since leaving Detroit on my journey South, about how things change with the passing of time and the absence of news (especially in time of war); and how I had met someone else and found a new direction in life. Yet before I could utter a word of any of it, I was cut off by a new disturbance as Marshal Gilson and another officer, Deputy Sheriff Jim Draper, appeared at the top of the stairs with guns drawn.

The marshal shouted: "Johnny Golden! I have a warrant to arrest you for murder."

Johnny raised his hands and nodded in surrender. In the almost palpable silence that followed, and with everyone in the room gathered around watching, Johnny said:

"All I ever wanted was just to see you again, Carlotta. You take good care now, you hear!" The deputy sheriff cautiously approached Johnny, took the pistol from his holster and shackled his hands with a pair of rusty manacles.

I looked at him quizzically. "You've changed, Johnny. What happened to you?"

He gave a sardonic chuckle. "War does things to you."

As Johnny turned around without resistance to be led away, he glanced back over his shoulder at me once more.

"I will always love you, Carlotta."

The crowd gave way on either side as the marshal led Johnny across the room, and his head disappeared down the stairs. It would be the last time I ever saw him. Alive, that is.

Despite my best efforts, I felt tears streaming down my face. A handkerchief suddenly appeared and dabbed my cheeks, and I looked up to see Frank. The expression on his face was, however, not one of compassion, and I dreaded to hear what he would say next.

But before either of us could say a word, the sound of gunfire broke out from the street below. Frank dropped the handkerchief and rushed to the window, and I got up and quickly followed. Directly below us, a crowd of people stood around a dead and bloody body stretched out in the mud.

It was Johnny.

23

"HE TRIED TO ESCAPE."

That was the only explanation offered by the marshal as we hurried up. He calmly replaced his pistol in the holster by his side as the deputy sheriff stooped down to pull Johnny's hat over his still-open eyes.

Frank said, "But his hands were manacled!"

"Don't make no difference," replied the marshal.

"Such men are dangerous. Besides, this'un here's wanted dead or alive. Don't much matter either way for the likes of him."

"There's a bounty on him, too, I'll bet," said Frank. "I don't set much store by this brand of vigilante justice."

Marshal Gilson glared at Frank before gesturing at me. "Well, now, by the looks of things, I just done you a big favor, mister!" The deputy sheriff and several of the onlookers laughed. Frank's face turned red as a summer rose at that. He gave only a curt grunt in reply, then turned away without so much as acknowledging me and disappeared back into the saloon. I looked back to the marshal.

"What will you do with the body?"

"Same as we always do, we'll bury him out back of the churchyard."

I opened my purse and counted out about sixty-five dollars and handed it to the marshal. "This should cover his funeral expenses, including a coffin and a proper suit to bury him in. Please see that it is done."

Marshal Gilson looked surprised as he took the money. "Yes, ma'am!" he said. I turned my back on the grisly scene and made my way down the avenue toward home. Frank and the Bee Hive would have to do without me for now.

I did not attend Johnny's funeral, thinking it best to distance myself from the whole affair as tongues were wagging enough as it was. But from my window later that afternoon, I could just see the churchyard in the distance, where a pauper's grave was already dug for

Johnny's body to be interred without further ceremony apart from the perfunctory recital of the Lord's prayer by the local minister. He was a Methodist and the only man of God to be found in those parts, and I had not seen fit to inform him that Johnny was Jewish. They might not have afforded him a proper burial at all (leastways not in the churchyard of a house of God) had they known that detail about him.

I could see the marshal and a few other people standing around the grave as Deputy Sheriff Draper and another man lowered the wooden coffin into the hole while the minister went through his motions. When it was over, I suddenly fell into a fit of weeping. I could not fathom from where in my soul such deep emotions had welled up to burst into a flood of tears, but maybe it was because I felt I was somehow to blame for Johnny's death. I also knew my last link to my youth and home was now irrevocably broken forever. There was no going back to any aspect of my past, and there was nothing for it now but to join the irrepressible forward march of time. To this future belonged my love for Frank, but I feared even that was now lost. If so, I would be lost along with it.

I had steeled my nerves for the inevitable confrontation ahead, though my dreaded walk to the Bee Hive among gawking eyes was spared by the appearance of Frank at my door. It was already late in the afternoon when he arrived, and a patina of burnt orange light had formed on the adobe wall across from the window. The warm glow belied the cold draft that blew in when Frank entered.

If I had hoped the first thing he would do would be to embrace me with the reassurance that everything was all right, I was sadly mistaken. Instead, he strode inside without a word and stood for what seemed an age in front of the small fireplace warming his hands. I just sat at the little table and watched him in silence while waiting to hear what he had come to say. Finally, he turned and stared at me for a long moment with what I perceived as a look of disappointed resolve.

He said, “Everyone at the saloon is talking about you and that Johnny boy.”

“People will talk.”

“That all you’ve got to say about it?”

“What else is there to say?”

“You might tell me why you never said anything about him to me.”

“I did not reckon on it being of any import.”

“Not of any import? That you were woman to a murderin’ outlaw was not of any importance to me?”

Frank reached down and tossed a log onto the fire, then grabbed the black iron poker and angrily stoked the glowing coals.

Before he spoke to me this way, I had thought to explain things, to tell Frank that what had happened was long ago and that I was responsible neither for Johnny’s actions nor his pursuit of me. But after his hurtful words, I felt defiant.

“You’re sure one to talk, Frank! Last I looked, you were something of an outlaw yourself for murdering a man in cold blood in San Antonio. That’s why you’re here now and not still back there with your family. And using an alias to boot, just as I must do for your sake!"

"I killed that man in self-defense. And to save you, I might add!"

"I don't need saving, I can take care of myself!"

"Well hell, Carlotta." Frank shook his head. "Fine then, next time, I'll just leave you to fend for yourself."

"Fine, then." I rolled my eyes the way that always got Frank's goat and stared into the fire.

"Don't you roll those pretty eyes at me, sugar! Let's see how you manage around here without a decent man to look after you."

I knew as I said it that I should not have said what I said next. Yet I could not help myself.

"I reckon there are plenty other men around. And there's not a one in this place that seems any more decent than the other. In fact, I have not observed any hint of decency among the menfolk around here at all!"

Frank gave an angry huff and gestured toward the window. "Look's like the only man you ever truly loved has found a permanent dwelling in yonder churchyard."

I gave a sarcastic chuckle despite the sudden bitterness I felt, and murmured: "Beware the green-eyed monster ..."

"Beware the what?"

"The affections of a jealous man I do not crave. And you're acting jealous over a dead man."

He turned back furious, and pointed at me with the sharp end of the fireplace poker. "I ain't jealous!"

Having seen Frank's volatile temper in action, this naturally alarmed me. Yet not enough to hold my tongue.

"Yes, you are quite frankly just being jealous over

nothing!" I could not help laughing at my own pun, though Frank did not see the humor of it. I added: "Jealous, and silly too."

"Silly?" He was shouting now and getting closer with that threatening poker. "You think it's silly that people say I am cavorting with a little cheatin' card-sharp whore?"

At that, I turned away in speechless disbelief and stormed to the door. I did not want Frank to see that he had brought me to tears.

"Where are you going, young lady?"

I did not answer as I reached for the doorknob, opened the door, and stepped out into the street, giving the door a good slam behind me for good measure.

It was already a cold twilight outside, and the first stars were out. I thought for a moment to rush back inside and grab my coat, but immediately thought better of it so as not to ruin the effect of having so dramatically walked out. I turned quickly to the right and walked into the long alley behind the row of shanties so that Frank would miss me if he tried to follow.

Sure enough, within moments, I heard his voice hollering to me from the front of the house. I picked up my pace, not thinking about where I was going. I only knew that I wanted out of that town and to go somewhere far away, someplace where I could feel safe and happy and loved and independent all at once. And it was clear that not a one of those things could I find there where I was at that moment. Perhaps no such place even existed. I had never felt so trapped.

Not, at least, until after what happened next.

I continued walking down the alley until I came to the last wooden shanty in the row, just before the riverbank. I was by now shivering and crossed my arms tightly for warmth. As I rounded the corner, I caught a momentary glimpse of a large hand in front of my face before I felt it cover my mouth with a painful slap. Another hand attached to a strong arm grabbed me tightly from behind around my torso. I heard my muffled voice cry out vainly for help as I strained my neck sideways to get a look at my captor. Then I saw him: It was the evil, one-eyed Comanchero I was warned about at the saloon.

He was not alone either. I now saw another man step out of the shadows toward me. This one tied a filthy rag over my mouth to gag me and then bound my wrists tightly together with a piece of rope behind my back while the first held me firmly in his grip. Then without a word between them, they dragged me down to the river, where a third man stood tending to three horses.

The first man now lifted me up and forced me roughly onto his horse. I tried kicking him, but before I knew it, he was up on the saddle behind me and spurring the horse forward along the river bank as the others followed. I felt something cold and sharp pressed against my throat.

"Sit still and quiet, or else," he whispered in my ear. His breath was foul.

By now, it was almost pitch dark, and I little hoped that Frank or anyone else would see me before I disappeared into the darkness with my abductors. With that thought, I was seized with a sudden terrible fear, wondering what would now become of me. For once, I had no ace up my sleeve.

24

WE RODE ALONG THE RIVER until arriving at a place where the banks narrowed. Here the Great Western Cattle Trail that continued through town as Griffin Avenue crossed the Clear Fork of the Brazos. And here the men slowed their horses and spurred them almost in unison into the swirling water to ford the river. By the time we reached the middle, it was so deep the horse I was on seemed near to swimming, and I felt the icy cold water slowly cover the length of my legs beneath the blouse of my dress that I knew would be miserably drenched for a long time afterward. Soon I felt a tug from beneath and knew the horse had found surer footing and was ascending up the farther bank. I found myself wishing a sudden torrent would rise up and carry me off into the current and put an end to it all. I knew this would be preferable to whatever these villains had in store for me.

But alas, no such help came from nature that night. The horses all arrived wet but safe on the other side, and it was there that the three Comancheros finally conferred together in low voices. The second man (who had earlier tied my hands), an equally unpleasant rogue with hair that fell about his neck in long, greasy strands, spoke first.

"Where to now, Bertrand? Direct to Fort Worth?"

"No!" replied the man behind me, clearly their leader. "Come morning, them Tonkawa Injun scouts they got at the fort'll stick to our tracks like butter on hotcakes. We'll ride northwest into the *Llano Estacado* a good ways first. Then we'll cover our tracks and loop over the top of the Clear Fork, and head east to Fort Worth from there."

I had noticed that the third man, a rather corpulent fellow in a broad sombrero and colorful poncho who seemed more suited to a mariachi group than to a band of bandits, was watching me intently in silence. Now he spoke.

"What about the girl?"

"What about her?" answered Bertrand. "We take her to Fort Worth and fetch a mighty fine profit, that's what! They trade whores right alongside horses there, where a fiery little mare like this'll have 'em eating out of our hands. We'll sell her to the highest bidder!"

The second man now eyed me with a lusty leer. "This mare needs breaking in first before sellin' her off. I reckon I can ride her!" He looked back at the third man and grinned. "Ain't that right, Tomás? I bet she can buck a tiger all right!"

Tomás chuckled. "Si, Bill. We can handle her!"

I felt Bertrand's hand squeeze my shoulder. It hurt. He said, "Whatever you fellas do, you best not damage her—else I'll damage you! They ain't buying nothing but the finest livestock for them fancy Dallas whorehouses."

At that, Bill took off his hat and leaned toward me from his horse in mock deference. "Don't you worry none, miss, we'll be real gentle with you. Every night till we get you to your new home. And we'll start tonight!" He began to dismount from his horse, but Bertrand's hand left my shoulder and gestured for him to stop.

"Not here! First, we ride a good piece till we get to them pinewoods just past that hill up yonder. There we'll make camp and light a fire, and you can have your fun. I don't figure anyone'll miss her until tomorrow morning, leastways. By then, we'll be long gone!"

Bill sat back up on his horse and nodded at Tomás with a wicked smirk. He spurred his horse forward, and the others followed. By now, I was shaking as much from fear as from the cold. I choked in a struggle to breathe beneath the tight rag over my mouth. I had never imagined such terror in my worst nightmares. I wished now that I had never left Kentucky at all, that I had ridden out the war with my mother and sister at the plantation and maybe found happiness by the end the way my sister had done. Now here I was, about to suffer horrible humiliation and torment alone in the wilderness, followed by an even worse fate enslaved in a Texas whorehouse. And all for what? My only reason ever to have ventured into the godforsaken frontier was out of my love for Frank. A love now forever lost over a trifling misunderstanding.

As much as I prayed for time to stop there and then, we soon reached the other side of the hill and came to the edge of the pinewoods Bertrand had mentioned. The sweet coniferous smell of pines was sufficiently pungent to reach my nostrils despite the stench of the rag beneath them and that of the brutish man behind me. That once beloved scent now only increased my fear as I recalled the men's plans for me upon reaching the woods. Nonetheless, some beautiful association of that pinewood scent took me back to a happier time and place in childhood memory—a time when, as a young girl, I played beneath the trees by the pond under the protective watch of my mother. I closed my eyes and struggled to hold on to the brief warmth of joy brought on deep inside by this memory, but the feeling was quickly dispelled when Bertrand snorted like a pig behind me and ejected a wad of tobacco spit that I heard splatter upon the ground beneath us. It took me back to the night in San Antonio when a similar ruffian had spat upon Frank's boot, only to be quickly dispatched to the eternal hereafter. This time, alas, my luck had run out. There was nobody now to save me.

We rode a ways into the woods in silent swiftness, apart from the light sound of the horse's hooves pressing upon a dense bed of old pine needles. A full moon was out, its light obscuring the stars above but shining through the trees with an eerie glow and casting long shadows. In any other circumstances, I would have found the scene beautifully enchanting. But not this particular time and place.

Not far into the woods, we came to a small clearing, and here the men halted.

Bertrand said, "We'll rest here a few hours, then set off before first light after some breakfast." He dismounted and offered me his hand. I refused to take it and looked away.

"Suit yourself, little hussy!" He reached up and grabbed me roughly then, pulling me down from the horse and dragging me to the edge of the clearing where he forced me to sit down atop a decaying log.

"You sit there and be still without a peep, you hear! Best not try to run off neither, as you won't get very far. Anyhow them wolves in these parts will get you if we don't!" As if in answer, a distant howl echoed from the distance.

"You hear that?" he said with a laugh.

The sound brought chill bumps of fear all over my body. Bertrand smirked and went back to his horse and came back with a blanket that he tossed over me.

He said, "No use you getting sick and dying before we can get you to Fort Worth." Then he walked over to help the other two start a fire. As I sat there watching, I tried to put on a brave face but inside remained terrified.

Before long, they had a good fire blazing close enough so that I could feel a little warmth. As I sat there shivering, I stretched my arms out behind me and wished I could move my hands to my front so as to warm them. I had never felt so cold and miserable.

Bill said, "Where's that worm of yours, Tomás?" Tomás uncorked a bottle of clear liquid, took a big swig, and passed it to Bill. I knew it would not be long now until the mezcal went to their heads, and they got to remembering their designs for me.

As I watched them, their faces appeared distorted in the flickering light, making their features twisted and grotesque like three monstrous trolls huddled around the fire. Sure enough, after a few more swigs from the bottle, Bill stared in my direction and pointed.

"Time for a little sport!"

He got up and took another long swig from the bottle before handing it to Bertrand and glancing back at Tomás, who lumbered after him in my direction. Bertrand remained by the fire and lit a cigar in the flames. "Don't forget what I told y'all," he warned, then added: "Enjoy your honey, boys. You've earned it!"

Bill now reached me and Tomás stood just behind.

"She looks a damn sight prettier in the dark now, don't she?"

Tomás laughed. "That's just the worm talking to you, Vaquero!"

"Well, let's see that flaming red hair in the firelight."

I tried my best to brace myself for what I knew was about to come, while vainly straining to free my hands and to plead for mercy with my stifled voice. My legs were still free, and I jumped up and tried to run but immediately tripped over a rock and fell to the ground. I looked up to see Bill hulking over me with Tomás gloating from behind. The men dragged me back toward the campfire, where Bertrand sat calmly smoking his cigar and staring into the blaze. I could smell the harsh cigar smoke mingled with that of the fire. Now I felt Bill's hand groping up my leg beneath my dress.

He said, "I'm gonna make you purr, honey. Purr now, purr like a pussy cat!"

I felt such a combination of fear and disgust that I instinctively kicked him hard between his legs. He howled in pain and grabbed his groin as I struggled again to get away until Tomás took firm hold of me from behind. I caught a glimpse of Bertrand chuckling to himself while puffing his cigar.

"Do not you move, señorita," Tomás growled in my ear. I felt the sharp point of a knife press into my neck as he nudged me toward Bill.

Bill was angry now. “That’s it, keep her still for me.” He reached out and took hold of Frank’s locket dangling from my neck and tossed it to the ground when the chain snapped. Then he unfastened his belt and opened his trousers before lifting my dress. “Purr,” he said again, moving close with his ugly erect body. “Let’s see you buck this tiger!”

I closed my eyes, resigned to the worst, as he grabbed my arms and continued taunting me in that awful voice. I could feel tears streaming down my cheeks.

“C’mon, honey!” he continued. “Buck this ti…”

His voice abruptly stopped, and he let go of me with a shriek. I felt the knife point lift off my neck, and when I opened my eyes, I saw Bill’s face contorted in pain and terror, staring down at his groin where blood spurted forth like a fountain. Something glinted in the firelight. Then I saw that it was an iron arrowhead. An arrow was sticking right through Bill’s privates!

“They got me through the pisser!” he yelled, as he writhed on the ground, cursing in his agony.

I heard “them” before I saw them. There was a sound of yelping and whooping from the darkness just beyond the clearing. Tomás pushed me aside and drew out a pistol, swinging it around fearfully in all directions. A shout came from behind. It was Bertrand, now running toward his horse.

“Kiowa!” he shouted. “Run!”

Tomás fired his gun into the darkness, panic-stricken. There was a whirring sound as several arrows found their home in his chest, one directly through his heart. He fell backward onto the ground. Dead. He was the lucky one.

The sound of hooves resonated as a small band of Kiowa warriors rode into the clearing, shouting their war cries. I was frozen with fear and could not move as one of them, a powerfully built man with braided hair flowing out behind him, rode toward me where I stood by the fire. He ignored me, however, focusing his gaze on Bill, who tried to run despite the horror of his affliction. The warrior brandished a knife as he leapt from his horse and grabbed Bill's long hair from behind, pulling his head back and scalping him with a motion that—despite its dreadful consequence—could only be described as an act of precision. Bill gave another tormented shriek as the warrior held up his scalp in triumph. Then he reached down and threw Bill headfirst right into the fire, pushing him down with a foot on his back into the hot coals. I thought no man could scream with pain the way he did then as the flames roared, until he finally went silent. However, I was mistaken. He would soon be outmatched by another.

Bertrand had disappeared on his horse into the darkness so that, in my naiveté, I thought he had gotten away. Yet here he came back, still on his horse but bound with rope and apparently uninjured. His captors had other plans for him.

Everything now happened very fast. One of the warriors—the one who had killed Bill— appeared to be searching the firelit ground nearby for something. He called excitedly to the others in their own tongue, pointing at what looked to be a small mound of dirt. Bertrand neither spoke nor struggled, clearly trying to remain stoic though I could see the fear in his eyes as he watched another of the warriors hammer two stakes into the ground with a rock. When they began to strip Bertrand, he finally struggled to get free. He looked quickly in my direction before dropping his head in shame at his complete nakedness.

The warriors forced him to the ground on his back with his arms stretched out behind, tying his hands and feet to the two stakes with his head near the dirt mound. He now pleaded with them.

"I have gold!" he shouted. "Let me go, and I can make you all rich!"

One of the warriors, who, with his headdress and elaborate war paint I took to be their Chief, replied in English.

"Where is gold?"

"In that satchel there, on my horse." Bertrand pointed with his chin to his horse standing nearby.

The Chief nodded, and another warrior opened the satchel and brought out a handful of coins. They gleamed golden in the firelight.

"We will take your gold, then you are free to go!"

"God-a-mercy!" Bertrand gave a smile of relief. But his smile quickly dropped into a frown as the warriors turned their backs to him and left him there to return to their horses.

"Wait!" he entreated. "You promised to set me free!"

The Chief turned back around and stared coldly at

Bertrand. "Free to go to the white man's hell."

The warrior who had scalped Bill now paced back to Bertrand carrying a leather pouch. From it he poured a thick liquid substance over Bertrand's body, starting with his face and on down the rest of his body and over his genitals. It appeared sticky. Then the warrior stooped over Bertrand's head and began rubbing the substance around his eyes and nostrils and even into his ears.

"There is your honey," he said.

He picked up a stick and pushed it down into the mound of dirt near Bertrand's head. The stick immediately appeared to come alive with a dark line of something moving upwards.

"Please, no!" Bertrand implored. "I beg of you!"

In response, the warrior raised back his leg and gave the mound a fierce kick, sending the ant-filled dirt all over Bertrand's face and body.

"Only cowards beg!" he said. Then he leapt upon Bertrand's horse and spurred it forward to rejoin the band.

If I had any hope they had forgotten about me and would just ride on away, that hope was quickly dispelled when the same warrior turned in my direction and scooped me up with one strong arm as if I were some trinket found along the way. He set me in front of him at my previous place on Bertrand's horse. Only this time, the man behind me was even more frightening. And he was sporting Bill's scalp!

The band of warriors turned away in unison behind the Chief to leave Bertrand to die a terrible death alone in the dark woods. It was some time before I could no longer hear his anguished screams echo through the woods behind.

I felt myself pitying Bertrand then, despite his intent to have made my life a living hell without a second thought. But I also knew that this was no rescue on my part. Far from it! I might have been spared the ravages of Comanchero bandits, followed by enslavement and forced prostitution. Yet despite it all, I had only gone, as they say, "out of the frying pan, into the fire."

But at that point, I must have closed my eyes and fainted, what with all the overwhelming fear and exhaustion I had felt. Afterward, I could remember no more of that awful night.

25

WHEN I OPENED MY EYES, there was sunlight streaming through an opening above me. I was alone but wrapped in warm blankets inside a buffalo-hide tepee, and there was food and water set nearby. The first thing I heard was a bird chirping. It sounded familiar, like something from my childhood beckoning to me, and I carefully peered through the flaps of the tepee to look outside. It appeared to be late morning already. There was a light scent of smoke in the air and the distinct smell of roasting meat. A little distance away, behind a large tepee, I saw several Kiowa warriors, including the Chief and the warrior who had made short shrift of both Bill and Bertrand before lifting me to his running horse, sitting around a fire roasting a deer upon a spit. Other warriors were moving about their camp within a copse of tall oak trees, and one tended to the horses tied up some distance from the firepit. One of the horses I recognized as Bertrand's. There were a number of women also, huddled by the fire and wrapped in long, colorful shawls. One of them nursed an infant. A dog of a kind I had never before seen trotted through the camp barking excitedly.

I heard the birdsong again and followed the sound to spot a redbird in the tree above. Just then, a ray of sunlight struck its feathers, and it glowed with a beautiful crimson color. It was the first one I had seen since reaching the frontier, but the "Kentucky Cardinal" had always been my favorite bird since I was a little girl, when my grandmother once told me they were a sign of good luck and meant the soul of a loved one was watching over me. Frank and I had seen one together in San Antonio, when he told me a Cherokee legend about redbirds. He said the Cherokee believed the redbird originally to have been born of the sun—and that the male got his color by painting himself red with the help of a wolf he had saved from a trickster raccoon's mischievous prank.

As I watched the beautiful bird singing carefree on his branch, the horror of the night before returned to my mind, and I cowered back inside the tepee, wondering what those fierce warriors had in mind for me. I did not have to wait long.

What happened next remains in memory like a dreamlike haze following the living nightmare I had endured, compounded by the return (and death) of Johnny and my subsequent fight with Frank. But by and by, I heard a new sound outside: the noise of hooves as of many horses approaching.

I looked back out to see the Kiowa warriors swiftly mounting horses. Some had bows ready, while others wielded guns. They watched in alarm as a regiment of blue-uniformed soldiers entered the camp on horseback. But what struck me immediately was that the soldiers were all colored. Buffalo Soldiers! Then I recalled that they were part of the 10th Cavalry Regiment garrisoned at Fort Griffin.

As I watched, a man who appeared to be their captain rode forward toward the warriors, his hand extending a white flag of truce. Riding next to him was both a horse and a man I immediately recognized. It was Frank! And it was he who now appeared to exchange some words with the Chief, followed by his handing over to the Chief what I recognized as a money sack Frank was accustomed to use for our winnings at the saloon. It appeared quite hefty. But once the money had changed hands, the Chief pointed in my direction, and Frank quickly spurred Nell and rode toward me. I recall little after that apart from falling into his arms with a feeling of elation such as I had never before imagined.

The last thing I remember is trembling as the warrior who had shown such violence the previous night—and who had made of Bertram a royal meal for the ants—walked toward me as Frank helped me mount Nell. But the warrior, whose name I later learned was Dancing Rabbit, was smiling as he extended his hands to me with a small and carefully wrapped bundle.

"For you!" he said.

When I looked closer, I saw that it was a little newborn puppy.

The next thing I knew, we were back at my place in Fort Griffin, where Frank tended to me with great care until I regained my strength. Though it would take some time before I felt sufficiently brave to venture forth alone again.

That first night back, Frank explained how a Tonkawa woman washing clothes in the river had observed my abduction by the bandits and quickly ran to tell her husband, who was a scout at the fort. Once Frank heard about it, he spent a sleepless night waiting anxiously for dawn, when he rode to the fort at first light to muster help. With the native tracking skills of the Tonkawa scout to aid them, Frank and a large unit of the Buffalo Soldiers' cavalry followed the bandits' trail until they discovered the fateful campsite in the woods.

When they arrived in the clearing, they saw the smoldering campfire with Bill's partly burned body sprawled in the ashes. Tomás lay nearby with arrows protruding from his chest.

Frank dismounted and picked up an arrow from the ground.

"Kiowa ..." he mumbled anxiously.

He looked up as a young soldier shouted nearby.

"Captain!"

The soldier was visibly disturbed at what he had found. Frank watched anxiously as the cavalry captain rode over and dismounted to look closely at Bertrand's body covered with crawling ants.

"My God," he exclaimed. "He's still alive!"

The captain took out his pistol, aimed it carefully at Bertrand, and fired. Frank then looked around in a panic for me.

The captain asked, "Any sign of her?"

Frank shook his head in despair. Then something shiny caught his eye, and he reached down to pick it up. It was my broken gold necklace with the locket he had given me. He opened it and found his own picture staring back at him.

Frank exchanged another quick glance with the Captain and jumped back on his horse, spurring her forward behind the Tonkawa scout as the Captain and soldiers followed. Not having found my body there, they traced the warriors' trail to the Kiowa camp near the abandoned old post of Fort Phantom Hill.

As we embraced that night in the light of my fireplace, I looked at Frank sternly.

"You were very ugly to me, Frank."

"I know, and I apologize. Please forgive me! And remind me never to doubt you again."

"Of that, you may be sure!"

He sighed. "Sometimes you have to lose what you love to realize what you had."

I looked at Frank tenderly and kissed him.

"I love you, Frank."

He reached into his pocket and drew something out. To my delight, it was my necklace and locket, which he had repaired and now slipped back over my neck. Then he kissed me sweetly.

"I love you too, sugar!"

PART VI

Aunt Lottie

26

FRANK AND I REMAINED in Fort Griffin for several more years. Time just got away from us. But during that time, business at the Bee Hive continued to thrive, and we were comfortable enough in what had become a daily routine. We often traveled too for a change of scenery, taking trips to gamble in towns such as Denison, Fort Worth, Dallas, Fort Stockton (home of my dear friend Annie Riggs) and even as far south as Brackettville—where there was easy money to be had in the saloons trimming the soldiers from nearby Fort Clark.

We got back to Jacksboro some too, where Shanssey still ran "The Little Shamrock" although he himself had previously removed to Fort Griffin as proprietor of the aptly named "Shanssey's Saloon." That is when I talked Frank into making an offer to buy the Bee Hive from Shanssey, who accepted. So we now ran the saloon and gambling resort as a thriving business ourselves.

I also invested in another local boarding house and saloon called "The Gus" for some money on the side.

I was later accused of "running a disorderly house," but that is of course nonsense, the kind of thing men always want to say about a woman who happens to be successful in her own right. Especially in that time and place. (Some even went so far as to accuse me personally of partaking in that sinful profession.)

By now, I had a clear understanding with Frank that our eventual marriage was most certainly, shall I say, "in the cards." Yet we also understood that such a future life together hinged upon removing ourselves from that godawful place, especially given the growing sense of desperation there—due in large part to the economic downturn following the decline of the buffalo trade. There was even talk that the fort itself would soon be closed down, now that the buffalo herds were decimated, and the Indians largely subdued and forced onto reservations following the recent Red River War. This, in turn, led to a collapse of local income from the hide trade that had fueled the growth of the Flat in the first place. One consequence of this desperation was a violent and deteriorating situation that had become near intolerable.

I had certainly begun to hanker for such a change, and I badgered Frank about setting out West as I had long dreamed—and he had long promised. He finally relented, and when the first chance came, he took a job as a local ranch hand and joined a cattle drive on the Great Western Trail that passed right through Fort Griffin on its way to Dodge City. After that, he hoped to find an opportunity somewhere in the New Mexico

Territory where we could move together. In time, perhaps, we might even stake out some good land where we could start a ranch of our own and, at long last, settle down together for good.

While he was away, I resolved to keep busy by winning as much as I could to help us in our move. I was grateful to have my dog with me. I had named her Ellie Mae in honor of my sister. She was by now fully grown and as rambunctious as might be expected from an Indian dog! Otherwise, I did not at all like being left alone in Fort Griffin, a place that had become ever more rough-and-tumble as time went by. Almost every notorious character from what they now call the "Wild West" passed through there at one time or another, and I had had the good fortune (sometimes misfortune) of encountering them all.

By May 1878, it was finally time to leave Fort Griffin and Texas for good. Frank had secured an interest in a new mine in the New Mexico Territory (which he had won over a game of poker) and had gone on ahead to Silver City. In the meantime, I was to make my way there alone as safely as possible—no easy task then, as rail travel was a few years off yet. My only option was once again to travel by stagecoach, with the lands in between still very much infested with bandits as well as vengeful Comanche, Kiowa, and Apache holdouts desperate to protect their vanishing territory and way of life.

As I prepared to pack up for the trip West, I found my old and dilapidated trunk would no longer do. I recalled, however, seeing an attractive leather-bound trunk in the possession of the young new Shackelford County sheriff from the county seat of Albany, a fellow Kentuckian by the name of John C. Jacobs.

When I approached Sheriff Jacobs about buying it, he offered to give it to me, but upon my insistence he finally accepted a token payment. It was sturdy though the leather was scarred and somewhat cracked, having accompanied him as a hide hunter on the buffalo range. But it had pretty brass trimmings with a solid clasp and was nevertheless light enough to facilitate travel. So I stuffed it full of my finest clothes (many of them long-unworn), along with quite a fortune in cash buried beneath them. This was no insignificant risk, as I knew full well. I also knew that the loss of my trunk and possessions therein upon the western road would most likely be accompanied by my life itself. Yet there was nothing else for it, as I was now once again determined to risk all for the chance to start anew.

Apart from the good sheriff (for whom I had concocted a story that I was leaving to rejoin a long-lost husband from my youth, who had finally located me and written with a plea to make a new start together out West), the only other people who knew anything of my plans were Shanssey and my old friend Emily, the doctor's wife. (I had sworn each to secrecy concerning my background, such as they understood it, and about my intention to leave.) Rather than call attention to myself by selling off my remaining possessions, including my little house—which I now owned, having bought it from old Mr. O'Connelly several years earlier—and some rather nice furniture I had collected over the years, I simply left a note inside to be found after my "disappearance" was eventually realized. It read: "Sell this outfit and give the money to someone in need of assistance."

On a beautiful morning on the twenty-fifth of May, Sheriff Jacobs kindly transported in his buggy me, my trunk, and my dog Ellie Mae to catch the Fort Concho stage headed southwest toward San Angelo and El Paso—and from thence beyond to the Territory of New Mexico.

For the first time in many years, I felt a twinge of excitement inside as I embarked once again on a daring adventure into the unknown.

27

IT WAS A GREAT DAY indeed when I finally boarded the western stage from El Paso. Suffice it to say, I have seldom felt happier than the moment my next stagecoach venture took me past a sign that read:

Entering the Territory of
New Mexico

Fortunately, the journey to Silver City passed without serious incident, leaving me to exult in the beautiful landscapes along the way. I had heard tales of the striking views to be had further out west, but nothing had prepared me for seeing this strange new world in person. I wish I had the words to give some idea of the wild scenery there, or to describe its beauties. With each mile, an even more beautiful view seemed to open as we wound in and among the hills with their rocky sides matted with grey moss and purple cactus. There were truly romantic mountains and deep canyons upon every side, with enchanting blue mesas beyond in the farthest distance. In one place, we even went through a narrow pass through the mountains that was entirely carpeted with wild roses. I often found myself wishing I could just stop and spend many days wandering with my dog through all of those wonderful ravines along the way.

Once we settled in at Silver City, life proceeded apace. In the years that followed, Frank invested (with mixed results) in mining claims, while also grub-staking miners and investing in local real estate interests. We also naturally continued to do what we did best: running saloons and gambling halls together. My favorite venture in those days was our place called "The Monarch," located in the back of the Victorio Hotel in Kingston, where we spent one very enjoyable year. For a time, I owned and managed the successful Broadway Restaurant in Silver City. We also operated a popular place there called "The Gem." It combined a saloon and gambling resort with a restaurant, dance hall, and variety theater—and was quite well patronized. I even acquired a new nickname, being known for a time in Silver City as the "Faro Queen."

By 1881 we had finally made our permanent home in Deming, where Frank eventually built a modest but comfortable house on West Pine Street. I made it my business to decorate our new home with the most elaborate furnishings we could find (and afford). We had a nice tree-shaded backyard for the dog, and our home was even noted locally as being the only house in town with a carpeted outhouse! We also had a small ranch around twenty miles outside Deming in the foothills of the mountains, where Frank raised cattle for a while.

We had from the start agreed to take up our rightful names again, too, feeling safe after so much time away from Frank's San Antonio past and eager to leave the aliases "Mike Fogarty" and "Lottie Deno" forever behind us in Texas. Frank's two brothers, Harrison and Will Thurmond, eventually joined us in Deming before becoming well-known gamblers out in Tombstone. They had decided to sell the old University Club and come out West after hearing Frank's tales (albeit somewhat exaggerated) of the riches to be had. Their parents were now deceased, and their sister Barbara Ann had married, maintaining with her husband the old family farm in Mississippi. Their other sister, Jenny Kate, had since reformed her ways and now ran a profitable boarding house in San Antonio. Meanwhile, Harrison had a family of his own now, too. He and his wife, Kate Thurmond, had a little girl named Hayley, our treasured niece, and for a while they lived in a house nearby.

As for myself, I adopted the more fashionable name "Charlotte" (my birth name), while nevertheless indulging Frank's fondness for "Lottie" as an enduring pet name. For the first two years, Frank and I lived together as a common law couple. But though this meant Frank called me his "wife" and I took his name—now happily calling myself "Mrs. Charlotte J. Thurmond"—I remained ever desirous of a proper marriage. I had, after all, just turned thirty-six and felt it was high time for Frank to make a true commitment of the matrimonial kind—especially lest something happen to him, and I find myself doomed to the dreaded state of "spinsterhood" (never a pleasant prospect for a middle-aged woman in those days).

But I finally got my wish with a little help from the law, for once: Given the constant influx of miners drawn by the recent strikes of silver and gold, the local population began clamoring over the lapse of public morality. A law was therefore enacted that decreed any people living together "as if they were married, and not being so, shall be considered as living in a state of concubinage." The threat of stiff fines for not immediately joining "in the bonds of matrimony" was sufficient motivation for Frank to finally join in such a bond with me. On the second day of December 1880—after some fifteen years of anticipation—I finally got my day in church!

Soon afterward, however, another life-long dream would end in tragedy. While I had long suspected that I was cursed with "a barren womb," Frank and I were overjoyed to learn one day that I was with child. We spent the better part of that year dreaming like a couple of young newlyweds of our domestic life to come, planning a fine nursery and looking ahead with anticipation of an heir to whom to devote our future work.

But it was all in vain. The child was born sickly, and she died within just a few short precious days. Before she died, we arranged for her to be properly Christened. (I named her Mary.) Yet I still treasure the newspaper notice of her birth published in the Silver City Enterprise, full of a promise and joy destined never to be:

"A daughter has been born to Mr. and Mrs. Frank Thurmond, of Deming."

The experience of such a tragic loss had a profound effect on both of us. Frank had become so enamored with the anticipation of fatherhood that he immediately sank into a dark stupor. In time, he found a new purpose in dedicating himself to helping local children and their education, including raising the necessary money to build the first school in Deming. Frank and I—along with our old Indian dog Ellie Mae and a ginger-furred cat named Miss Kitty—soon became beloved figures among all the local children, and we rejoiced in being affectionately dubbed "Uncle Frank" and "Aunt Lottie" by all.

For myself, after also suffering in a state of deep depression for a long while afterward, I finally "got religion" (or rather, rediscovered my strict Episcopalian upbringing) after attending a revival led by a preacher of fiery passion. This moved me sufficiently to become a founding member of the new St. Luke's Episcopal Church, to which cause I donated all of the old gambling money I had kept hidden in my trunk toward the new building. I soon helped start the first Sunday school there too.

I swore off gambling for good after that. Not Frank, though—he had never had much time for church and still did not, though he nevertheless professed good Christian values, which he demonstrated by joining me and the church in helping children and others in the community with charitable activities. Frank's advancing years did not, however, slow down his various antics. On at least two occasions, these landed him in serious trouble and nearly cost him his life.

One hot August night in the year 1884, Frank got into a drunken quarrel over a high-stakes billiards game with a man named Dan Baxter, known around town as "Silver Plate Dan"—seeing as how he said he had a silver plate in his skull to repair a fracture. (His subsequent autopsy proved otherwise.) Following their dispute, Baxter launched a billiard ball at Frank's head which—had it hit home—might have done lasting damage. Instead, it had the unfortunate result of provoking sufficient rage in Frank to produce his still-ubiquitous Bowie knife from behind his neck, with which he proceeded to cut his adversary badly in the abdomen.

Baxter died of his injury soon thereafter. Once again, Frank's bladework became the talk of the town, and he was soon arrested and charged with "Assault With Intent To Commit Murder." But his luck held when, after naturally arguing self-defense, the Grant County Grand Jury issued a "No Bill" in his case.

As if escaping a charge of murder were not enough, Frank pushed his luck yet further by robbing a bank in 1893. Though not without good reason. It transpired one day that the only bank in Deming was forcibly closed after a bank examiner discovered malfeasance during the annual audit. While counting the Deming bank's cash, he noted a particular $100 bill that was somewhat mutilated and had one corner burned off. The next morning, when this same examiner arrived in Silver City to inspect its local bank (owned by the same man), upon counting the cash there he was surprised to discover the same mutilated and burned $100 bill. The examiner immediately caught the train for the fifty-mile trip back to Deming and demanded to see the cash on hand, of which there was none. As the examiner suspected, all of the Deming bank's cash had been hurried by messenger the previous night to Silver City to make it appear both banks were financially secure upon inspection. The result was that both banks were promptly closed with all accounts frozen, frustrating depositors in both Deming and Silver City and thereby causing a general uproar.

Frank, who had $1,100 dollars in his account at the Deming bank, decided that this state of affairs simply would not stand. He somehow entered the bank, only to be adamantly refused his money by the clerk inside.

"Mr. Siebold," Frank insisted, "I have eleven hundred dollars deposited in this bank, and here's my withdrawal check. I want my money!"

"I am terribly sorry, Mr. Frank, but it is impossible for you to withdraw any cash at this time, not till the examiner releases it."

Frank said, "Perhaps you did not rightly understand me. Allow me to rephrase my request." He drew out his Colt .45 "Peacemaker" and pointed it at the astonished clerk, accompanied with that menacing look of his that brooked no quarter.

Frank's argument being now considerably more persuasive, Mr. Siebold quickly opened the vault and proceeded to count out the cash with shaking hands.

"Eleven hundred dollars, did you say?"

"Yep." Frank nodded and put away his gun. As soon as the money had been handed over, he tipped his old and by now quite fashionable Stetson hat to the man, along with a friendly "much obliged." Then he casually departed the bank as if he had just made a routine transaction.

Frank was arrested that same day and charged with bank robbery. But his luck held yet again when at his trial the judge ruled that while Frank's method for retrieving his money was admittedly "unusual," he was nevertheless within his legal rights to demand the cash that rightfully belonged to him. He could therefore not be charged with "stealing" what was his own. The case was summarily dismissed, and he was once again a free man. Frank was also the only depositor in either bank to ever get a penny of his money back.

He eventually became president of that same bank, the Deming National Bank. Leave it to Frank to become president of the very bank he had once robbed at gunpoint! (In my life with Frank, there was never a dull moment.)

It was not until the year 1908 that Frank's luck finally turned in the wrong direction. Up until then, he had somehow always found a way to beat the odds. From brushes with death during wartime to his various close calls with fellow gamblers and with the law, he always had an ace up his sleeve. Yet, in the end, he met the one adversary whom he knew to be his match.

One day in the spring of that year, while smoking his pipe, he felt a sharp pain in the back of his mouth and throat with no apparent cause. He naturally figured it would just go away on its own, but with each passing day, the pain seemed to grow worse until it became unbearable even for Frank—a man who had always taken pride in his ability to withstand any kind of hardship. His visit to the doctor confirmed our worst fear: Cancer.

After his diagnosis, the disease progressed quickly, until Frank was largely confined to bed. Everything that could be done to relieve his pain was attempted, though ultimately to no avail. Then an abnormal growth appeared in his throat. According to the doctor, Frank had one final hand to play, in the form of a surgical operation to remove the tumor. The surgery itself was successful: The growth was removed, and Frank soon made a full recovery despite the shock of his operation.

But after years of cheating Death, this time the cards were stacked against him. To use another old—yet, for Frank, quite apt—gambling cliché, he had been dealt a losing hand from which no bluff could save him. Within a few days, the growth reappeared, resulting in the doctor's prognosis of death within "weeks or days."

We resolved to make the most of our remaining time together on this Earth, especially as Frank was at least able now to move around the house and even to sit with me outside under the blooming vines of wisteria in our cherished garden. During this time, he never uttered a word of complaint, despite the pain I knew he suffered, along with the knowledge of imminent death. Just ten days later, he was back in bed—this time we knew for the last time.

On his deathbed (at home, where he wanted to be), Frank waxed philosophical at the very end, despite the painful struggle it was for him to speak.

"I don't reckon," said he, "that humanity would amount to a hill of beans if all we did with our precious time was to waste it making money."

I squeezed his hand and gave him what must have been a bittersweet smile. "Then what did you and I ever amount to, my dear?"

"Why, a whole heap of love, my darling!"

Frank stared at me thoughtfully for a moment with those deep hazel eyes of his. "A whole heap of ..."

His voice faltered, but he gave me the warmest smile I had ever seen before his eyes glazed over into a blank stare. At that moment, I felt his hand go limp in mine.

Frank's face quickly blurred behind the veil of tears in my eyes, as I bent down to kiss him one last time.

"Of love," I whispered.

EPILOGUE

The Golden Gossip Club

IN HIS WILL, Frank made me his sole beneficiary, leaving me with sufficient means to live modestly but comfortably. For over twenty years now, I have devoted my life primarily to my circle of loyal friends and to my church. I also teach a popular Sunday school class, where I include lessons in Hebrew based on my memory of studying it at the Episcopal convent of my youth. I even helped form a new social club in 1912 that counts many of the most prominent women in Deming as members. It is called the "Golden Gossip Club," and to this day, I have never missed a single weekly luncheon meeting.

We gather on Tuesdays to play bridge with matchsticks on my front porch (I always win). We sew quilts, crochet church altar cloths, and swap recipes—my old New Orleans Creole recipe book proved quite a hit with the ladies! Most importantly, of course, we gossip about all of the latest goings on about town.

I also take occasional vacation trips to various parts of the country in my newfangled Ford Model T automobile. While I have often thought of returning to Kentucky to look up my family there, for some reason I always think better of it. After all, I would be hard-pressed to explain myself and to account for my sixty-year absence! Last I heard, my sister Ellie Mae was widowed, though with several surviving children to look after her. I suppose they might wonder sometimes whatever became of the "Aunt Carlotta" they never knew. In looking back on my long life, my only regret is that of losing touch with family and friends along the way—including my sister and, of course, Mary. (I so often wonder whatever happened to Mary, and can only pray that she, too, wound up happy.)

That is, after all, what led to my writing these memoirs: The hope that maybe someday—long after I am gone, of course, to preserve my "innocent" persona among the good folk of Deming—my family back home and their descendants might learn my true story. If so, may they take comfort in knowing that, after my long journey, I found genuine happiness in the end.

I did, after all, finally realize my dreams of finding both love and the respect afforded to a proper lady in society. I had come full circle from the days of my youth on a prominent Old South plantation. Oddly enough, Mama and Daddy might actually approve of how I turned out. Though what an adventure it was getting here in the meantime!

I had hoped against hope with nothing much to lose. But I put my faith in Frank, and he—in his inimitable and roundabout way—came through in the end to help make my dreams come true. Yet I also learned this: It is up to each of us individually to find our own keys to happiness. Dreams come true to those who understand the things for which they dream.

In my Last Will and Testament, I have dictated that I wish to be interred next to Frank at his final resting place in Mountain View Cemetery in Deming. I have further directed that I am to be buried with my headstone just back of the left shoulder of his own.

There I shall remain as Frank's "lookout" for the eternal hereafter.

About the author,

FRANK THURMOND

FRANK THURMOND grew up in Little Rock, Arkansas, and holds graduate degrees in English from Southern Methodist University and Oxford University. His previous books include the memoir *Before I Sleep: A Memoir of Travel and Reconciliation* (2012, Et Alia Press), a collection of short fiction titled *Ring of Five: A Novella and Four Stories* (2015, Et Alia Press) and his poetry chapbook *Remembrance and Other Poems* (2022, Braddock Avenue Books). In addition to writing, he is a musician and an award-winning filmmaker.

He teaches literature, composition, music and screenwriting at the University of Arkansas at Little Rock. In his spare time, Thurmond enjoys serenading his two rescue dogs with his Renaissance lute.

Thurmond was inspired to pursue his creative interests in writing and music after a serendipitous discovery as a graduate student researching Renaissance Drama at Oxford University. While studying Renaissance lute music and performance as part of his research into the original music in Shakespeare's plays, Thurmond learned that his 17th-century ancestor, Nicholas Lanier, also played the lute and served as "Master of the King's Music" for King Charles I. This connection led to Thurmond's being invited to perform lute music for Queen Elizabeth II and Prince Philip during their visit to Oxford in 1999.

Further research into his Lanier ancestry led to Thurmond's finding direct kinship with other writers and musicians, including the 19th-century Georgia poet and musician Sidney Lanier and celebrated playwright Thomas Lanier Williams (aka Tennessee Williams).

The desire to try his hand at writing a "literary Western" novel found inspiration through Thurmond's friendship with the late author Charles Portis, especially after reading a copy of the novel *True Grit* personally inscribed for him by Portis. Soon afterward, a friend's chance observation online of a photograph of the historical Frank Thurmond led to the suggestion of writing a novel about this 19th-century namesake—who, as it turned out, was an ancestor from the same Thurmond family. Upon researching this character further, however, it quickly became clear that the real story was that of the fascinating woman known as Lottie Deno (the historical Thurmond's real-life lover); it is thus her story that became the focus of this book.